Dear Readers,

Many years ago, when I was a kid, my father said to me, "Bill, it doesn't really matter what you do in life. What's important is to be the best William Johnstone you can be."

I've never forgotten those words. And now, many years and almost two hundred books later, I like to think that I am still trying to be the best William Johnstone I can be. Whether it's Ben Raines in the Ashes series, or Frank Morgan, the last gunfighter, or Smoke Jensen, our intrepid mountain man, or John Barrone and his hardworking crew keeping America safe from terrorist lowlifes in the Code Name series, I want to make each new book better than the last and deliver powerful story-telling.

Equally important, I try to create the kinds of believable characters that we can all identify with, real people who face tough challenges. When one of my creations blasts an enemy into the middle of next week, you can be damn sure he had a good reason.

As a storyteller, my job is to entertain you, my readers, and to make sure that you get plenty of enjoyment from my books for your hard-earned money. This is not a job I take lightly. And I greatly appreciate your feedback— you are my gold, and your opinions do count. So please keep the letters and e-mails coming.

Respectfully yours,

William W. Johnstone

WILLIAM W. JOHNSTONE

BLOOD BOND
SLAUGHTER
TRAIL

PINNACLE BOOKS
Kensington Publishing Corp.
www.kensingtonbooks.com

Following the death of William W. Johnstone, the Johnstone family worked with a carefully selected writer to organize and complete Mr. Johnstone's outlines and many unfinished manuscripts to create additional novels in all of his series, like THE LAST GUN-FIGHTER, MOUNTAIN MAN, EAGLES, and others. This novel was inspired by Mr. Johnstone's superb storytelling.

PINNACLE BOOKS are published by

Kensington Publishing Corp.
850 Third Avenue
New York, NY 10022

All Kensington Titles, Imprints, and Distributed Lines are available at special quantity discounts for bulk purchases for sales promotions, premiums, fund-raising, and educational or institutional use. Special book excerpts or customized printings can also be created to fit spe-cific needs. For details, write or phone the office of the Kensington special sales manager: Kensington Publishing Corp., 850 Third Avenue, New York, NY 10022, attn: Special Sales Department, Phone: 1-800-221-2647.

Pinnacle and the P logo Reg. U.S. Pat. & TM Off.

First Pinnacle Books Printing: June 2006

10 9 8 7 6 5 4 3 2 1

Printed in the United States of America

PROLOGUE

He loved it. Loved the look on their faces. Loved the fear in their eyes.

All he had to do was walk past them, the delightfully whippy split-bamboo flail in his hand, and they cringed, knowing they might be the target, knowing they would indeed be the target. This time, next time, sooner or later the flail would seek their flesh.

Oh, how fine it was, the flail. He'd had it for years. Intended to have it always. When first he found it the flail was the color of pale, sun-washed sand, a light tan tinged with yellow. But that was long years ago. Now the wood—was it wood? he was not entirely sure what bamboo should be considered—now the slender, springy sections carried a lovely, varnishlike patina, the color of a golden sunset with an underlying shade of red.

Very appropriate the red for it was put there by the frequent and copious application of blood. The blood of cowering men. He liked the sound and the feel and the sight of the bamboo stinging their flesh. Splitting it open. Bringing the blood until their backs ran red with it. Until the flail took on its color.

Even more than the blood of men, he reveled in the blood of the women. Terrified women. Screaming women.

It was an odd fact, he mused. When he cut men with the precious flail, they hunkered down in fear or stood boldly in defiance, but either way they were almost always silent when the welts were raised and the flesh split apart.

Women, though, the women screamed. They begged. They wept loud and bitterly. They asked for mercy.

The flail had no mercy.

Nor did he.

Case Wilhelm smiled as he passed among them, smiled as if in benediction.

He held the wonderful, four-and-a-half-foot-long flail lightly in one hand while he looked, while he chose, while he decided which of them would provide an example for the others to learn by.

Ah, yes.

That one!

Wilhelm's smile became wider as he altered his direction and took a firmer grip on the flail.

He began to tremble with anticipation. The flail, the power were his. The only thing that could make this better would be if he had a woman to castigate and to educate— he liked them the best—but at the moment all he owned were men.

That man, however, would do. He would do nicely.

Case walked faster, the flail rising and falling with the pumping of his arm.

He raised his hand, the flail poised above the chained man.

With a whirring sound that was to him the sweetest of music, the flail so sharply descended. . . .

CHAPTER 1

"I'll race you to the square."

"If we do that we will get fined."

"So they fine us a dollar each. So what? Let's make that the wager. Loser pays both fines, how does that sound?"

"Excellent. And for you, I will make it simple. Go ahead without me. You win. I'll pay your dollar. How is that?"

"You're no fun today," Matt Bodine accused.

Sam August Webster Two-Wolves yawned. "What I am today is tired. Fortunately I know how to cure that. When we get to the hotel I'm going to take a bath, have a meal served at a table, and then go to bed. Wake me in about two days. Then I'll think about a race if you still want to. A footrace, though. These horses are probably as tired as we are."

"You always win those," Matt observed.

Sam Two-Wolves's handsome face split in a huge grin. "Why do you think I want it to be a footrace, brother?"

Matt shook his head. And held his horse to a walk. Sam was probably right. The horses were too tired from travel to be forced into a run through the narrow lanes and few thoroughfares of Santa Fe.

For more than a year the two, brothers by choice rather than birth, had been drifting, for the time being simply enjoying their youth and their freedom. Soon enough they would tire of exploration and want to settle down on the ranch land they owned in Wyoming. But that time was not yet. At the moment they were happy wanderers, enjoying the country, enjoying meeting strangers and making friends of them, enjoying each other's company.

Matt Bodine and Sam Two-Wolves had been as close as brothers ever since the long-ago day when, as boys, Matt saved Sam's life. Matt was the son of a Wyoming rancher, Sam the child of a powerful Cheyenne chief and a highly educated woman from a wealthy Boston family. Since that day the two boys had been as close as brothers, spending time in each other's homes, until Matt was ceremoniously made a blood brother of the young Cheyenne and accepted into the tribe as if he were one of them.

Matt was educated at home by his mother, a former teacher, while Sam went East to attend college. When Sam returned to Wyoming the two resumed their close friendship as if there had never been a separation.

The boys, now men, even looked alike, each standing over six feet tall and with a large, powerful frame. Matt had brown hair and blue eyes while Sam's hair and eyes were black, but otherwise they could well be mistaken for brothers by birth.

They also happened to be exceptionally gifted shootists, adept with their Colt revolvers both as to speed and accuracy. Matt might have been a hair quicker with a gun, Sam slightly more accurate. Between them they were a formidable fighting machine. Or could have been. They were much more interested in enjoying life than in furthering the reputation that was already spreading about them.

At this moment they were returning to Santa Fe, which like Denver and Kansas City and a very few other places was among their favorite stops in their travels. When chance took them near Santa Fe they generally managed to find some excuse to stay a few nights at La Fonda, the handsome hotel on the public square just a few steps away from the Governor's Palace. Returning to Santa Fe and La Fonda felt almost like a homecoming to them.

The narrow lanes wound past walled, adobe houses and dusty pens doing a haphazard job of containing goats and donkeys, chickens and ducks. Eventually the two men broke out onto the broad wagon road that was the end of the fabled Santa Fe Trail. They followed that into the heart of the city, and tied their horses at the hitching rings outside the fine old hotel where the likes of Kit Carson and Jedediah Smith once stayed. It was rumored that Jesse James visited there more than once as well, but if he did it was under an assumed name and no one seemed to know for sure.

One thing they could be very sure of was that they liked La Fonda and looked forward to their stays there.

The clerk at the little office cubicle in the lobby recognized them when they entered. He began to smile in welcome. "Hola, young gentlemen. Will you be wanting the same rooms as before?"

"That sounds just fine, Jose. An' some hot bathwater as quick as you can get it up there."

"Of course, Mr. Bodine, Mr. Wolf. Welcome." Jose never had quite gotten a handle on Sam's name and for reasons unknown always abbreviated it to Wolf. Jose, an assistant to the manager, turned and motioned to a boy, who quickly darted near and relieved both Matt and Sam of their saddlebags and bedrolls. Another youngster was dispatched to see to the needs of their horses, and a platoon of bellboys hurried away to fetch tubs and buckets of hot water for the baths.

"A fella sure can feel pampered around here," Matt observed.

"Do you mind being pampered?" Sam asked.

"Not me. I was only making note of it, not complaining. No, sir, they can pamper me all they please an' probably then some. I'll suffer through it in silence."

"That's what I like about you, Matt. You are so brave."

"Yeah, I kind of think I am too," Matt answered with a grin.

The two collected the keys to their adjoining rooms and turned toward the stairs.

"Oh, wait, please. One moment," Jose said before they were more than two steps away. "I almost forgot."

Jose disappeared into the hotel office. He was gone for only a minute. When he returned he was carrying a soiled and much-traveled envelope. "This came addressed to either one of you gentlemen. It has been here for more than a month, I think, maybe two, maybe longer." He handed the envelope to Sam, who happened to be standing closer to him.

"Mail? Who would be sending mail to us? And how would they know where to find us?"

"From all the chicken scratchings and postmarks on this envelope," Sam said, "I'd say that it went to your father first and he forwarded it. Looks like it has made several stops since then."

"Well, don't just stand there. Open it."

"In the room. I want to get these boots off and sit down for a change on something that isn't moving. We'll open it there."

"Want me to read it to you?" Matt prodded while they headed to their rooms.

"No, thanks. It always bothers me how your lips move when you read," Sam told him with a grin.

"Hurry it up then, will you. My curiosity's up."

"Keep your britches on, white boy. Remember that patience is a virtue."

"I never claimed to have any virtues. Now hurry it up, darn you."

Sam was laughing when they reached their rooms, both of them turning in at the room Sam preferred.

"Oh, my gosh," Sam exclaimed. "I almost forgot about this fella. But then you always knew him better than I did."

"Who?"

"Pete."

Matt's eyebrows shot up in inquiry.

"Peter Branvol. Remember him?"

"Of course I do."

When Matt and Sam were boys still learning the ways of each other's culture, Peter Branvol was a cowboy working on Matt's father's ranch, a laughing, happy-go-lucky youngster in his early to middle twenties, probably not far then from the age Matt and Sam were now. He more or less adopted the two, teaching them the finer points of roping. And if the truth be known, teaching them to enjoy the crisply bitter flavor of beer as well. He took the two boys under his wing and contributed to their education.

"I haven't thought about Pete in years. How about you?"

Matt shook his head. "He worked for my dad just two seasons. I looked for him coming hiring time the next year but he never showed. Never wrote to me either."

"I got one letter from him after I went back East to school," Sam said. "He was encouraging me, said I could make it in the white man's world if I didn't have a chip on my shoulder." Sam smiled. "My mother had already told me that, of course. I always kind of wondered if she put Pete up to sending that letter."

"She could have," Matt said. "He rode with me a time or two when I went over to visit with your folks. So why is he writing now? And how did he find you?"

"Us. It's addressed to both of us."

"Then why are you reading it?"

"Because I'm the one with the college education. Now be quiet and let me look at this, will you?"

I herd about your reputionn with a gun. Herd you helped some folks up to Colorado one time. I want to hire you. Cannot pay much but I need help. I am married now with a little boy and nuther coming. Got a place SW from Nogales in Sonora State, town called San Iba. I need help.

                                        Your friend,

                              Peter James Branvol.

"This was mailed more than two months ago."

"I wonder if he still needs help."

"So what do you think?"

"You know good well what I think. I'm thinking the same thing you are."

"We're already gotten rooms and it's getting too late to travel today. I say we have those baths and a good sleep, then we'll ride out again at first light tomorrow."

"Just what I was thinking too. Now all we need are those bellboys with the tubs and the hot water."

CHAPTER 2

"I need a bath," Matt complained.

"I can agree with that statement," Sam told him.

"You're one to talk."

Sam sighed. "I would argue the point except that it is true. We both need baths."

"I sure enjoyed the bath I had back in Santa Fe."

"It seems a long time ago, doesn't it," Sam mused. The two were sitting beside a very small fire at the foot of a low, rugged mountain northeast of Tucson. The comforts of La Fonda seemed very far away. Their supper had been stick bread and bacon, both roasted over the flames. The coffee was starting to boil now, its aroma spreading to the pine-scented night air.

"Uh-oh," Matt said under his breath, his head coming up and his eyes flashing.

"Stay here."

Matt nodded, but by then Sam Two-Wolves had already disappeared into the night, going as silently and as quickly as if he were evaporating on the moving breeze.

Matt reached for the coffeepot, poured himself a cup, and rocked back on his heels with the cup held under his chin so he could best enjoy the smell of it in anticipation of the flavor.

"Got enough here to share if you'd care to come out of that brush and sit with me," he said without raising his voice.

After a few moments a man wearing ragged clothing pushed his way into view, pine needles crunching and tiny twigs snapping underfoot as he bulled his way through a clump of scrub brush. The man needed a shave and the services of a seamstress, but there was nothing unkempt about the carbine he held aimed in Matt's direction. The weapon looked clean and properly cared for.

"I only have one spare cup," Matt said as he motioned for the fellow to help himself to the coffee.

"Only need one."

"What about your partners there?"

"I'm alone."

"Mister," Matt told him, "there are three of you. You right there. Another fellow standing right over there. And the third gent is crouched down beside that rock yonder where he likely thinks I can't see him."

"You got good eyes."

"Good ears too," Matt said. "You three make as much noise in the woods as a bunch of bull elk in the rutting season. I heard you coming five minutes ago." He took a sip of coffee and nodded his approval. Smacking his lips, he said, "You really ought to put that gun down and have some coffee. It's a mighty good pot if I do say so."

"We didn't come for no coffee," the visitor growled. He lifted the muzzle of the carbine menacingly. And looked a little disappointed to see that Matt did not seem particularly menaced.

"Suit yourself," Matt told him. "But it's good coffee."

"Quit stalling. You know what we want."

Matt reached up with his left hand and tipped his hat back, then transferred the coffee cup to that hand. He took another sip, sighed, and set the cup down beside the fire.

"Don't stand up. Don't reach for that gun. Don't do nothing. Just give it up. Everything. Drop the gun belt, empty your pockets, and step back. We'll be taking what we want an' then move along. Don't give us no trouble and you'll still be alive when we leave here."

Matt seemed to think that over. He pondered the comments in silence for a moment, then nodded. "Yes, I can see that I will still be alive. But will you?"

"What? Mister, what're you talking about?"

"I'm talking about you and your partners," Matt said. "I've offered you coffee, nice and friendly. Now I'm offering to let the three of you go."

"Let *us* go? Bub, you're the one has got three guns pointed at you right now."

"Two," Matt said.

"What's that?"

"Two guns. You and your partners are down to two guns now. My brother has already disarmed the one by the rock there. He would have been the hardest to get lead into, so he had to go first. The thing I don't know is whether he's just knocked out or if it was better to kill him. That would have depended on how things looked when my brother reached him. If he had a protected position there he likely had to be killed, but I'm not sure about that. We'll find out directly, won't we."

"Brother? What brother?"

"The one you didn't see when you were trying to sneak up on us."

"You're bluffing."

Matt shook his head. "Actually, mister, I am not. And

if you push this thing, I will have no choice but to shoot you. My brother will shoot that other fella over there."

"I am standing here with a rifle gun aimed at your belly from a distance of ten feet an' you are squatting there with nothin' but a coffee cup in your hands. An' you say you are gonna shoot *me?*"

"That's right," Matt said agreeably. "That carbine of yours is not cocked. Before you can pull that hammer back and trigger a shot I'll have lead in you."

"Nobody is that fast."

Matt's look was chilling. "I am."

"You can't . . . ," The fellow raised his voice. "Jerry," he called into the night. "Answer me, Jerry."

"Jerry's the one by the rock?" Matt asked.

"I . . . *Jerry!*"

"Put your gun down," Matt said softly. "You can still have that coffee and be on about your business. Whatever it is."

The would-be robber's eyes went wide and the skin at his temples tightened and pulled back. Matt could see it coming, but he had no power to change anything. And no choice.

The fellow's thumb rolled back on the hammer of his saddle carbine.

Matt's hand flashed and the roar of his Colt shattered the peace of the evening.

A .45-caliber lead slug thudded into the hollow at the base of the robber's throat. His head snapped back and his knees sagged.

A second shot from Matt's .45 landed just to the side of his nose. The shape of the man's head distorted and there was a spray of wet gore shining briefly in the firelight.

At virtually the same instant another muzzle flash

outside the camp sent a sudden glow of light over the nearby brush as Sam's revolver discharged.

Sam too fired twice from a position close to the rock where the third man had been hiding. Another muzzle flash flared in the brush a moment before Matt heard the sound of a body fall to the ground.

"Are you all right?" Sam Two-Wolves called.

"Yeah. You?"

"He must have had his finger on the trigger. Jerked it when my bullet hit him."

"It's a shame they didn't settle for the coffee." The welcome aroma of boiled coffee had been replaced now by the sharp brimstone scent of burnt gunpowder.

"You make terrible coffee, Matt, but even I admit that it isn't so bad that a man should die to avoid having to drink it." Sam's voice faded as he moved away through the darkness. Several minutes later he came back into the firelight. "Bad news," he said.

"What's that?"

"The shot that fellow fired? It clipped your horse's nigh hock."

"Bad?"

"Bad enough. I'm sorry, Matt. The bone was shattered. I had to put him down."

"He was a good horse."

"More to the point, he was half of our transportation. I can't carry you double all the way down into Mexico, and Pete's letter was worrisome. It has already been several months since he mailed it. It sounded to me like he needs help fast."

Matt thought for a moment, then grunted. "I'll tell you what I think we should do. We'll ride double until we get down to the road. I'm fairly sure there is coach service along there. You can drop me beside the road and you get on down to San Iba. I'll catch a ride into Tucson, buy a horse there, and follow just as soon as I can."

"That could put you a couple days behind me."

"If you have a better idea I'd be glad to hear it."

Sam shook his head. "No, under the circumstances I suppose it would be best."

"Come on then. Let's drag those fellows clear of the camp. In the morning we can take a few minutes to cover them with rocks and brush or maybe find a slope where we can spill some loose gravel down on them. We'll read over them before we go."

Sam nodded, then hunkered down beside their dying fire and reached for both the cup he had abandoned there and the pot of coffee—very good coffee despite his complaints—that Matt had made.

CHAPTER 3

Matt had begun to think he was wrong about finding traffic on this road. The sun had already passed its zenith and was sliding down toward the western horizon before someone finally came along, and then it was not the public coach he'd been expecting but a rattling buckboard with a woman and two small boys in it. He had started walking toward that distant horizon several hours earlier and was dusty and footsore.

He set his gear down and stepped out into the road so the lady would have little choice but to either stop her team or run him over. She looked at first like she would elect to trample him under the feet of her two browns, but at the last moment she pulled them to a halt. Matt touched the brim of his hat respectfully, then took it off and held it in both hands.

"Ma'am. I'm surely glad to see you. I wonder could you give me a ride to the nearest settlement? I'm afraid I've lost my horse." He smiled, one of his twenty-four-karat smiles that was pretty much guaranteed to melt the heart of any young lady, even a married one such as this.

She looked nervous, so he pointed to his gear piled

beside the twin tracks of the road and added, "A body just hasn't any notion how much stuff he's carrying until he's the one carrying it himself."

When even that didn't appear to sway her, he ratcheted up the intensity of the smile another notch or two and said, "I'd be happy to pay for your time and trouble, ma'am."

The older boy, who looked to be nine or ten, nudged his mom's elbow and whispered something to her. The lady's expression did not soften, but her posture did. A little.

"My husband is not with us," she announced, as if he could not see that plain as day.

"No, ma'am."

"Are you a married man?"

"No, ma'am, I'm afraid I haven't the privilege of finding my life's companion yet," he answered.

The boy whispered to her again.

"It would shame me to ask payment for a simple kindness," she said.

"You never asked for anything, ma'am. I offered," Matt reminded her.

"I, uh. . . ."

"It'd be a true kindness," Matt said. "I am a stranger in need."

"Well. . . ."

"Please, Mama. He says he'd pay!" The boy turned his attention to Matt. "How much you gonna pay, mister?"

"Why, I don't know. How far is it to town?"

"It's pretty darn far," the kid said.

"Jason! It is not." The lady looked at Matt. "It is only a few more miles really."

"My feet tell me that's a few miles I'd rather not walk. I'll pay you anything within reason, ma'am, and be glad for your help."

"Then put your things in the back and get on. You can let the tailgate down and set on that if you like." Which would keep him as far away from her and her boys as it was possible for him to get and still be riding. He took no offense. She did not know him from Adam's off ox.

"Thank you, ma'am." Matt tugged his hat on and hurried to get his saddle, bedroll, and saddlebags.

The springy boards at the back end of the little wagon would have made a splendid diving board for jumping into the swimming hole back home, but every time the rig hit a good bump Matt felt like he was going to be thrown off. He would have felt considerably better if he had something to wrap his legs around and dig his spurs into.

The lady had been telling the truth about the distance, though. A small town—not Tucson but some outlying community—came into view within five miles or so. Matt swiveled halfway around so he could get a look at the place as they approached it.

The town was not much for size, but it made up for that by being drab, dingy, and weatherworn. All in all, Matt felt, it would be a fine place to be from. Far from.

Still, if there was a horse here that he could buy, he would be grateful. He wanted to get started after Sam Two-Wolves at first light on the morrow if that were possible.

He spotted a large barn at the near edge of town that was probably a livery barn. If so, there was a good chance his transportation problem could be resolved before supper.

He turned further around and said, "Ma'am, you could drop me—"

Before Matt could finish the sentence, however, there was a flurry of hoofbeats and two riders came pounding out from behind the livery. The lady shrieked and the smaller of her two boys began to scream. The older child, who would scarcely have stood waist high on either rider even if the newcomers had been afoot, jumped to his feet and lifted his little fists like he was ready to do battle. With both of them at once.

"Move aside," the lady shouted once she got herself back under control. "Jason, you sit down. At once, do you hear me. And not a peep out of you either, Derek," she snapped at the smaller child, which sent him into near hysterics. "Mr. Voss, Mr. Trudell, I will thank you to move out of my way. At once, if you please."

"What if we don't please?" the larger of the two drawled with an insolent sneer. The man was probably in his middle thirties, heavily muscled, although with a telltale bulge above his belt that suggested soft living and easy work. The gun tied down on his left thigh hinted at the sort of work that might be.

His partner was a few years younger and a little leaner, but looked to be in the better shape of the two. He too wore a revolver like he fancied himself a top hand with a gun. His holster was held down with a strap and buckle instead of a plain thong, and the leather on belt and pouch was tooled in an oak-leaf-and-acorn pattern. Matt suspected a fancy gun belt like that would set a man back a month's wages or more.

Both wore their hat brims tugged low. And neither offered the common courtesy of tipping those hats to the lady.

"Mr. Dwight wants you to sign that paper he gave you, Delia," the older man said. "He said I'm t' bring it back with your mark on it or he'll know the reason why."

"The reason there will be no signature," the woman called Delia responded, "is because I am not selling. Not now, not ever, and not at any price he could come up with." She set her lips in a thin line and nodded her head for emphasis, the movement abrupt and unequivocal. "Now I shall ask you again, Mr. Voss. Move aside. I have business in town."

"Goin' to the bank, are you? They won't loan you no more money. I can tell you that right now, Delia. You got no choice. You're through here. With or without that signature, Mr. Dwight intends to have that miserable little place o' yours, so's you might as well take the money he's offered. It's either that or you'll be put off with nothing in your pockets but lint." Voss grinned, an expression that lacked any hint of mirth.

"You leave my mama alone," Jason shouted.

"Shut your yap, kid, else I take you over this saddle an' lay my quirt acrost your backside."

"Leave my sons alone," Delia said. The words were brave enough, but there was a quaver in her voice now, and Matt could sense the rise of panic in her.

Matt stood up in the back of the wagon. He was smiling, but there was no more friendliness in his expression than there had been in Voss's.

"Who are you?" Voss demanded.

"Just a passing stranger," Matt said, his voice and manner easy although his blue eyes had turned to ice.

"Then keep on passing by, mister. You got no dog in this hunt, so don't be foolish an' get yourself all busted up for nothing."

"Or worse," Trudell put in. "Push us and you could get yourself shot down dead."

"I never did have much sense," Matt said cheerfully.

"What's that mean?"

"It means that I decline your advice."

"Huh?"

"I'm stepping in on the lady's side of things. Now

turn around like good little fellows and go tell your boss that Miz . . . ma'am, forgive me for being bold, but what may I say your name is?"

"Borden," she said. "Delia Borden."

"Thank you, ma'am. I'm—"

"Your name is mud, that's who you are," Voss snarled, "and you are a dead man or soon fixing to be."

"Excuse me, ma'am, but would you mind driving over there out of the way, please." Matt hopped down to the surer footing of the ground, leaving his gear in the back of the buckboard. He did not know how these horses might react to the sound of gunfire, and did not want to worry about keeping his footing in the back of a moving wagon while there was lead flying around.

"Now, boys," he said pleasantly. "Let's us three discuss this situation."

CHAPTER 4

"You got one last chance, mister. This ain't your fight. Turn and walk away now while you can."

Matt only shrugged.

Voss nodded to his partner, and Trudell tossed his reins to the larger man and dismounted.

"Last chance, mister," Voss said. "This here is James Trudell. He's the fastest gun there is, and if you don't leave be, he will show you just how fast he can be."

"I appreciate the advice," Matt said. "Now I will return the courtesy, and my advice to you would be to leave that lady alone. The both of you and your boss. Leave her be. Permanent."

"The only thing permanent," Trudell said, "will be the marker we put over your grave. What name do you want carved on it?"

"Bodine," Matt said softly. "Matt Bodine."

Trudell blanched, his skin suddenly pale and sweaty. "I . . . I . . . , uh. . . ."

"If you aren't going to draw, friend, I suggest you unbuckle and drop 'em. Just to make sure there is no misunderstanding. I just hate mistakes, don't you?"

"Look, I, uh. . . ." Trudell bent over and began frantically digging at the thin strap that held his holster tight to his thigh. He managed to get it off, then undid the belt buckle and let the whole affair fall into the dirt. He held his hands wide from his body and backed two paces away.

"Jimmy? What's the matter with you?" Voss demanded, his voice sharp with anger. "Why'd you go an' do a thing like that?"

"You never heard of Bodine and Two-Wolves? Well, I have. I ain't dumb enough to fool with them."

Matt gestured toward a well that stood in the shade of the livery. "Let's all of us walk over there, shall we? Mr. Voss, you can come down off that horse, please. Or drag iron. I don't much care which."

Voss looked confused.

"Ben! Get *down,* will you?"

Voss rather reluctantly stepped down from the saddle.

"Give those horses to Mr. Trudell, please. Ah. Thank you. Now if you would be so kind, I'd like you to drop your gun belt too."

Voss looked at Trudell, who was still sweaty and gulping for breath. "Do it, Ben. Please."

The big man handed the reins of both horses to James Trudell, then unbuckled his gun belt and eased it to the ground.

"Thank you, gentlemen." Matt picked up both belts and carried them to the well. Without ceremony he tossed them in, James Trudell's very expensive rig along with Ben Voss's plain one. There was a perceptible delay before he heard a distant splash. "That seems to be one problem solved, doesn't it," he said.

"Like hell it is," Ben Voss roared. "You're the next thing gonna go down that hole."

The big man balled his fists and lowered his head.

He charged straight at Matt, blood in his eye and with his hackles raised.

Matt stepped quickly to the side to avoid the rush, but Voss proved to be a better fighter than gunslinger. The big man was ready for Matt's maneuver and adjusted for it, lashing out with a roundhouse left that caught Matt on the point of his right shoulder, numbing that arm and making him wince with the sudden pain.

Voss whirled and came in again. Matt danced lightly to his right. His left fist shot forward, impacting high on the side of Voss's jaw. Voss stopped and pawed at his face, shaking his head as if to clear it. Matt stepped in and hit him with the left again, high, and then—stepping forward so the two men were nose to nose—whipping a hard uppercut that snapped Voss's head back and glazed the big man's eyes.

Matt threw the left again, an underhand blow to the pit of Voss's soft belly. Voss doubled over and Matt clubbed him behind the ear, driving Voss to his knees with a trickle of blood running out of his ear. The big man clutched his middle and began to vomit into the dirt. It took no special abilities to see that he was done with this fight.

"Stop! Stop this."

Matt spun around. His right hand was still virtually useless as feeling had not yet begun to return to his arm, but neither James Trudell nor the handsomely dressed man who was running toward them would likely know that.

Matt splayed his fingers wide and pumped his right hand into fists over and over, trying to encourage feeling. Trudell was little threat with his fancy pistol rig at the bottom of the well, but the newcomer was armed.

"Stop."

"Watch yourself, Mr. Dwight. This is that Matt Bodine fella. He's faster than a snake with that gun, and he just whipped Ben and only used his left hand to do it."

Dwight skittered to a halt and gave his two employees a dirty look, then shifted his attention to Matt. "I want you to work for me, Bodine. I can use a man like you."

"Oh, I kind of doubt that, Mr. Dwight. I kind of think you and I come down on the opposite sides of the fence here."

"We don't have to. . . ."

"Oh, but we do," Matt corrected him. He nodded toward Delia Borden, who with her boys in tow was coming to join them now that Dwight was on the scene. "You see, Mrs. Borden and I are going into business together."

The idea caught the lady as much by surprise as it did Dwight. Both parties looked confused.

"You want something that the lady here doesn't want to sell," Matt said. He smiled. "As it happens, I already owe her a little money. So I think what I am gonna do here is get her to sell me whatever it is that she doesn't want you to have. And I will hire her back to, um, run it for me."

"You don't even know what it is but you want to buy it?" Dwight asked incredulously.

"Exactly," Matt told him. "In fact, Mrs. Borden and I can walk right over there to the post office and get a bill of sale notarized and mailed off to the clerk of whatever county this is. That will make me an official partner in the deal and you won't be able to get hold of it, or put her off of it, without my signature on the deal." Matt's smile became even wider. "And mister, if you thought you were having trouble getting her to knuckle under, just wait until you try and force me into something."

"I just want . . ."

Matt stopped him with an upraised palm. "Mister, I don't even want to know about it. But Mrs. Borden and I can discuss any propositions you might make. Maybe she would want to offer a deal where you could sort of rent whatever it is you're wanting. If it wouldn't interfere with her. And if it brought it a tidy flow of income. Which she would also administer on my behalf." The smile turned into a grin. He turned to Delia Borden. "How are we doing with this, ma'am?"

"I . . . he wants to own the rights to a spring on my property. I can't let it go. I depend on it to water my garden and help keep my chickens. I need that water."

"But do you need all of it?"

"Well . . . no. Perhaps not."

Matt turned to Dwight. "Make the lady . . . I mean, make *me* . . . an offer if you want the use of some of that water."

"I suppose, um, I suppose I could run a cross-fence that would allow my stock to drink from one side of the pond there."

"What do you think that would be worth to you?"

"As it is, my cattle have to walk mighty far to water. It keeps them from gaining like they should. With water closer to hand, I would think"—he paused to consider for a moment—"I could pay ten dollars a month for the privilege."

"Twenty," Matt countered.

"The added weight gains wouldn't be worth that," Dwight said. "Could we compromise? Would she . . . that is to say, would you . . . accept fifteen dollars each month?"

"Year round?"

Dwight nodded. "All right. Winter and summer alike."

Matt turned to Mrs. Borden and lifted an eyebrow. The lady began to cry. "You don't know, Mr. Bodine. You don't know what you have done for us here."

Matt looked back to Dwight. "I'd say you got yourself a deal. You can pay the first month's rent now. Mrs. Borden will be collecting it for me, you understand. And mister . . . it wouldn't set well with me if I had to come back here and sort things out a second time. Like if I ever hear that you aren't living up to your end of the bargain. Do we understand each other?"

"I, uh, I believe that we do, Bodine."

"Good. Now if you will excuse me, sir, the lady and I have to go conduct some business so's I can get on about my own affairs."

Matt stepped over beside the wide-eyed and obviously adoring little boys and guided them toward their mother's buckboard.

Nice family, he was thinking. He wondered just how much he ought to pay them for the ride in to town. And for the property he seemed to be buying this afternoon.

Three days later the proud owner of a newly acquired small farm somewhere not far from Tucson sat in a café eating supper, a notarized bill of sale safely executed and in the mail. He was pleased with the way it turned out. Both parties would benefit, and Dwight had clipped the wings of his overly eager employees who, he said, overstepped their authority when they decided to use physical intimidation to get what was wanted. Matt believed the man when he said that. Pretty much.

That was the good news. The bad was that he still had

to find a decent horse. There had been only two nags available at the livery stable and neither of them looked like they would have the stamina for a trip that could prove to be hard and fast.

He had bought the better of the two, but had no intention of keeping it, not one minute longer than it took him to find a mount with some heart and some bottom to it. Surely he could find a good horse somewhere in Arizona Territory, but until then Sam was drawing farther and farther ahead. By now he could even have reached Pete's ranch at San Iba.

He . . .

Matt froze in the act of picking up his coffee cup. His hand began to tremble and a bolt of . . . something. . . . Fear. Anxiety. Something shot through his chest and roiled his belly.

Sam! Sam Two-Wolves was in danger. Matt knew that as plain as if he were sitting beside his blood brother instead of being in a café countless miles away.

Matt came halfway out of his chair. Then, wincing, forced himself to sit back down again.

Whatever was wrong, whatever the danger, Sam would have to face it without Matt's help.

For now.

Sam's lips thinned in a tight smile and his normally stoic expression softened. Teach your grandmother to suck eggs, boys, he thought when he saw the ambush beside the road ahead of him.

He was close to the border, although in truth he could not have sworn exactly which side of it he was on at the moment. The roads here meandered more than a little, and there were customs tax agents and livestock inspectors stationed only in the border towns. No one bothered to patrol—or really care—in the countryside.

The problem with that was that it made the border a potentially unhealthy place for travelers. Some could be waylaid almost with impunity for, whichever law a victim turned to, the criminals could claim they had been in a different jurisdiction at the time of the crime.

Sam had even heard, possibly with tongue in cheek, but conceivably with a grain of truth hidden within the yarn, that one trio of bold holdup artists had been recognized by a victim and reported to the Mexican authorities. The crooks were duly arrested and charged. When they came to trial, they swore their attack took place on United States soil. A Mexican judge dismissed the charges in the face of that confession.

The victim, not to be denied, demanded that the prisoners be turned over to U.S. civil authorities, and an exchange was made at the border crossing in the center of the town.

A second trial was held, and this time the prisoners swore on a stack of Bibles that their admitted crime occurred in Mexico.

And again the charges were dismissed for lack of jurisdiction.

Border justice, Sam reflected, seemed to be a sometime thing best handled on the spot.

Which was what he intended in this case.

But goodness gracious, one would think if these boys intended to make their living by way of pillage and robbery, they would at least learn to do it right.

There seemed to be two of them and at the moment they were talking to each other. One of them was wearing a pale yellow straw hat and the other a snow white felt hat. Neither one was particularly well hidden and when they talked they bobbed their heads. Sam could see the brims of their hats bobbing up and down like a pair of white hens pecking corn in a barnyard.

No doubt these old boys thought they were going to pull off a surprise when their latest victim came nigh.

Better luck next time, Sam thought.

He held his pace steady until he was almost opposite the two idiots, then hauled his reins over and gave his horse the spurs.

A Cheyenne war cry tore out of his throat as Sam, standing in the stirrups and flogging his horse with his hat, charged straight at the pair of inept highwaymen.

Sam took the reins in his teeth and drew his revolver, blasting bullets a few feet over the heads of the startled crooks.

Both men leaped to their feet and ran. One dropped the rifle he had been holding, but never so much as slowed his headlong flight. The other, just as terror-driven as his partner, kept falling down, crawling frantically forward on hands and knees for a few paces, jumping to his feet, and falling again.

If it hadn't been so serious, Sam would have found their ambush to be hilarious.

All right, he conceded. It was funny.

He chased the two for a good forty or fifty yards before he gave up the sport and reined down to a walk.

Sam returned to the road, not even bothering to go back to the ambush point to look for that fallen rifle. And somehow he doubted the weapon's owner would be going back for it either.

Sam hoped whoever found it was in need of the few dollars a used rifle would bring.

Sam's dark face split into a smile again as he continued

on the road to San Iba, and his belly shook with barely contained laughter.

The horse was not a bad one. Exactly. But it was not a good one either. The gaits were all right, but it did not have the stamina its build suggested it should have. Matt suspected it might have been wind-broken when it was young. He hated to delay, but decided in the long run he would be better off taking the time to swap for a better animal.

Besides, he did not feel so much urgency about Sam any longer. Whatever happened, Sam was all right. For now.

A sign hanging slightly askew proclaimed that the ugly little mining camp Matt was approaching now was called Tombstone. It seemed a strange name, and Matt was not sure if he even wanted to hear the origins of a name like that. Still, the place was bustling with activity. Money was being made here, and that was an event that was sure to draw a crowd of folks wanting to dip their fingers into the trough. There just might be a decent horse for sale.

Matt weaved his way through ore wagons and pedestrians, steered wide of a medicine wagon that had drawn a crowd, and headed for a narrow building made of laid-up mud bricks with a tattered canvas tent laid over the top of it for a roof. A sign out front read EATS. That and the flow of men drifting in and out said this was a place Matt wanted to go.

He reined to a halt and stepped down from the saddle with a groan. He and the poke-along horse had been on the road for hours, and if the horse was as weary as Matt, then it needed a break.

He let the animal drink from a nearby public trough,

then tied it outside what was left of a small building that had burned down. Matt stretched his back and pounded a little road dust off his clothes and headed for the café. There were some mighty mouthwatering smells coming out of the place, and he gathered there was a good reason why it was popular.

Matt stopped just short of the entrance, though, and snatched his hat off, standing and staring like a moon-struck kid when a gleaming phaeton rolled past carrying a vision from heaven.

The girl on the forward-facing seat was . . . elegant. Lovely beyond measure. She wore a tiny hat pinned at an angle above a cascade of dark gleaming curls.

And she was beautiful.

There was a man in the phaeton with her, but Matt scarcely registered the fact. It was the girl . . . Lordy, she was a beauty . . . who captured his attention.

A girl like that. . . .

"Oh! Excuse me."

"No, it's my fault," the tall gent said. The two had just collided at the doorway to the café.

Matt stepped back to allow the gentleman entry into the café. He smiled and shook his head. "Sorry, but I expect you know why I was staring," Matt said.

The gent grinned and said, "I was doing the same thing. Couldn't help myself." He scratched somewhere deep inside his mustache and shook his head. "You know, I think I might just have to marry that girl."

"Just from seeing her drive past?" Matt said. "Friend, my brother accuses me of being a romantic, but I'd say that you've got me beat all hollow."

The tall, handsomely dressed man laughed. "I'm not all that easy, son. No, that there is Miss Josephine Marcus. She came to town with a troupe of actors and decided to stay. The man with her is our local sheriff, Johnny Behan. She's smitten with him, but it won't last. I know Johnny and he isn't worthy to polish her shoes, much less court her. And his intentions are not serious. I'm certain of it."

"And yours are," Matt said.

"Oh, yes. The lady has my heart, no doubt about it."

"Well, I wish you luck, friend." He started for the door at the same time as the other man and again the two bumped into one another. Both laughed.

"We really do have to stop meeting like this, don't you think?" Matt said.

"I know how to resolve it," the gent said. "Join me for supper. Food always goes down better when you have someone to share it with." His grin appeared again, hiding inside his full drooping mustaches. "And if you are my guest, why, I must defer to you and allow you entry before me, isn't that so?"

Matt laughed. And led the way into the café. He stopped inside the door and let his host choose between the two empty tables, dropped his hat onto one of the unused chairs, and helped himself to a seat.

Despite the place being so busy, a waiter hurried to greet them. "Good afternoon, sir," he said, nodding at Matt, then turning his attention to the tall man. "Evening, Marshal."

"I'll have my usual order, Glenn, and bring my friend whatever he wants."

"Something solid," Matt said. "Meat and potatoes. I've been eating my own cooking lately and I'm not fussy."

"Very good, gentlemen. It won't be long." The waiter dashed away and Matt turned his attention back to his host. "Marshal did he say?"

"Just a deputy. My brother is the marshal." He

extended his hand across the table to shake. "Earp is my name. Wyatt Earp."

Matt shook the lawman's hand and said, "I've heard of you. Used to be up in Kansas, I believe."

"That's right, but there is something about the desert that I've always been drawn to."

Matt introduced himself and Earp said, "I've heard your name too. You're developing a reputation, Matthew Bodine."

Matt made a face. "It isn't something that I want, Wyatt." He shrugged. "You know how it is."

Earp frowned and nodded. "Indeed I do, but peace can be hard to come by."

"Can I ask you something?"

"Of course."

"Were you serious about marrying that lady?"

"Josie? Oh, yes. Serious as can be." He smiled. "It is just that she doesn't know it yet. And neither does Johnny Behan. I hope there won't be bad blood between us because of it, but I intend to have the lady regardless."

Matt believed him. Earp made the statement as simple fact and not as a tease.

Their meals came, a thick and aromatic stew served with corn bread, and Matt had a moment to look at this man who was a generous host. The most striking thing about him, apart from a clear and steady gaze, was his hands. He had a gambler's hands, with long, slender fingers and carefully pared nails. He wore a flat-crowned black hat, which lay on the seat of a chair at the moment, a black cutaway coat and vest, and a tie with a small pearl stickpin.

He was a handsome man this Wyatt Earp, approaching his middle years now. Matt wished him well in his pursuit of the much younger Josie . . . had he said her name was Marcus? Matt thought so. A couple such as that would be striking indeed.

It occurred to Matt that it was just as well that neither had taken offense out on the sidewalk when he and Wyatt bumped into one another. And when Matt was so openly eyeing the girl Wyatt intended to wed.

Matt had no doubt that he would have prevailed if he'd had a showdown with Earp—a man had to believe that in his gut or he had no business strapping on a gun to begin with—but he was more than pleased that it was not necessary to prove it.

He took another mouthful of the stew. Goat, perhaps. Whatever it was, it was good.

CHAPTER 5

Sam Two-Wolves was hot when he rode into sleepy, sunbaked San Iba. He was dusty. He was tired. He needed a bath, a meal, a drink, and a haircut. And he needed to get directions to Pete Branvol's ranch. But first he needed to get all those other things tended to.

It was late enough in the day that he could justify stopping now. The ranch could be many hours away, and there was no point in blundering around in the dark in country he did not know, looking for a place where he had never been. Better, he thought, to stop now. He could get a fresh start in the morning when he would be fresh as well.

Sam reined his horse to a halt in front of a low, rambling barn and set of corrals that he took to be a livery or freight yard. The town was only a few blocks long, so he would be able to walk from here.

A dark-haired boy who looked to be eight or ten came outside and stared at the lean, travel-worn stranger on his doorstep.

"Hello," Sam said, flashing a cheerful smile. "I need to put my horse up for the night."

The boy responded in Spanish.

"English?" Sam asked. "Do you speak English?"

The boy only looked at him.

Sam gestured toward the horse, then the barn. He made hand motions as if he were stripping the saddle off the animal, rubbing it down, and feeding it. This time the kid responded with a nod. He came forward and took Sam's reins and led the horse inside.

Sam thought about grabbing his saddlebags and bedroll, then decided he could come back for those. They should be safe enough here. He watched the boy and horse disappear into the barn, then began a weary walk into the heart of what passed for a town here.

At least half of the people he saw on the street, he noticed, were white, so Sam's lack of Spanish should not be a problem. Obviously this place, so close to the border, accommodated Americans. That probably had something to do with Pete's choice to live here.

Sam stepped up onto the sidewalk in front of a two-story building with a sign advertising it as the Cattleman's Inn. The hotel was set back from the street a dozen feet or so. The distance was taken up by a low roof with some sort of flowering vines climbing up the support posts. Tables, chairs, and a few rocking chairs were set on the paving stones that served as flooring. Sam was grateful for the shade. It almost seemed cool beneath the overhang. Strings of bright beads hung from the lintel over the doorway, placed there to keep flies out. Sam pushed through them, the beads clacking together noisily when they fell back into place behind him.

"Hello." He smiled at the man, white, who sat behind a low counter in a corner of the broad lobby. "I'd like a room, please. And bathwater. Do you serve meals as well?"

The man looked up, his face cold and unwelcoming. He scowled at Sam, then returned his attention to some papers on the counter.

"Excuse me," Sam said, reaching the other side of that counter. "I said I'll be needing a room. This is a hotel, isn't it? The sign says that it is, but I suppose I could be mistaken about something."

The man glared at him but still refused to speak, and after a moment stood, turned pointedly away, and walked into a back room, leaving Sam alone in the hotel lobby.

Mystified, Sam shook his head. He did not want to make a fuss about it, though. Everyone had a right to be as odd as he wanted. Including this fellow.

Sam went back outside, into the stifling heat of late afternoon. The air was not moving and the heat lay over everything like a particularly thick blanket, making even the simple act of breathing an effort.

There was a saloon close by where he probably could get something to eat as well as a beer to cut the dust in his throat. The saloon was built of lumber, as was the hotel. An adobe-walled cantina was in the next block. Sam assumed the cantina would cater mostly to the locals and he might have difficulty there because of his lack of Spanish. He entered the saloon instead.

A handful of customers were scattered though the room, a few at low tables and the rest standing at the bar. They wore wide-brimmed felt hats rather than straw, along with boots and spurs. Surely one of them would know where he could find Pete.

Sam stepped to the bar. He removed his hat to let a little air reach his scalp, smoothed his hair back with one hand—he really did need that haircut, he realized—and resettled the hat in place.

The bartender looked up and Sam said, "Hello. I'd

like a beer, please, and something to eat. And I'll be needing some directions too."

"You want directions? I'll give you directions. The door is over there." The man pointed. "Use it."

"Pardon me?"

"You heard me. This is a decent place. Your kind ain't welcome."

"My kind?"

"You heard me. Get outa here. Now!"

"Mister, all I want is a drink and something to eat, that and directions to a friend's place. Is that too much to ask?"

"Out!"

Sam's expression turned cold. "Mister, I asked you real polite. Now I'm telling you. Draw that beer or I'll come over to that side of the bar and get it myself. And you won't like it when I walk all over you to do that."

One of the men standing at the other end of the bar broke into the conversation. "Do what the man says, Tim. Pour him a beer."

"But . . ."

"Just do it, Tim. We don't want no trouble. If it makes you feel any better, I'll buy the beer. That way you won't be breaking the law. All right?"

The bartender did not look happy about the compromise, but he nodded and drew a beer.

"Thank you," Sam said. "But what law would it break if. . . ." He was speaking to an empty space. The man who had just interceded on his behalf had already walked out of the saloon, apparently without hearing Sam's thanks.

Sam shrugged. He could find the man and thank him later. Right now. . . . He buried his nose in the foam that was threatening to overflow his mug and drank down a long, throat-cleansing swallow of the crisp, almost bitter beer.

He drank that, and was about to ask for a refill and some food when he heard the clatter of boots on the puncheon floor as half-a-dozen uniformed Mexican soldiers pushed their way into the saloon. The soldiers carried long-barreled rifles made even longer by the gleaming bayonets that were attached. An officer, resplendent in epaulets and gold braid, followed close behind the soldiers. The officer carried a sword unsheathed in his hand.

The officer barked orders in Spanish and the soldiers—there were eight in the squad, Sam saw now—formed a line facing the bar. The Americans who had been drinking in the place hurriedly left, slipping out behind the soldiers.

Sam was about to do the same when the officer said something else and the soldiers first presented their arms, then turned slightly and, moving as one, snapped the rifles into position for a bayonet thrust. It was really a very pretty maneuver, Sam thought, although he would have enjoyed it even more if those bayonets were not pointed toward him.

"Surrender yourself," the officer ordered in heavily accented English.

"Me? What did I do?"

The officer gave another order in Spanish and the men began shuffling forward, their boots stomping loudly—deliberately so, Sam was sure—with each footstep.

Those bayonet tips looked wickedly sharp.

"If you're gonna kill him, Antonio, take him outside first, will ya? I don't wanta have to clean up a bunch of blood," the bartender pleaded.

"Surrender!" the officer ordered.

Sam looked at the officer, then at the bayonets, then at Tim the bartender.

With a shrug he held his hands out wide. There was nothing to be gained by a show of stupid bravado here.

Under the officer's direction two of the men set their rifles aside to come forward. They were not gentle about removing Sam's gun belt and binding his hands behind his back. When he was safely trussed, they shoved him into the center of the room so that he was surrounded by the soldiers.

The officer and two of the men were behind Sam. He heard a whisper of movement, then felt a hard, dull impact on the back of his head accompanied by a sound like that of a melon being broken.

After that he neither heard nor felt a thing.

CHAPTER 6

Sam Two-Wolves woke feeling like his head had been split completely in two and that now the two separate pieces were competing to see which could hurt the worse. He was lying on a stone floor, and must have been there for some time because the stone had more or less warmed to his body temperature underneath him. He tried to touch his pounding scalp so as to investigate the damage there.

Tried. That was all. Tried. He could not reach up that high.

His hands, it seemed, were shackled, locked into steel manacles that were linked by stout chains. The chains rattled when he moved.

Sam sat up. He managed, but it took him several tries. He was weak and dizzy. It did not help that his feet were chained too, wrist chains and leg chains joined by yet another length of chain. By sitting cross-legged on the floor and bending low, he was able to get one hand high enough to touch the back of his head. He could feel crusted blood there, but not as much as he would have expected from the amount of pain. If there was any good news, it was that he did not feel any shifting bone under his probing fingertips. The skull seemed to be intact, even if painful.

Satisfied at least about that, he was able to give some attention to his surroundings. He was in what surely was a jail cell with stone floor and stone walls. The cell was no more than six by eight feet. A steel door closed off one end. The only furniture was a wooden bucket that lay on its side in a back corner. The ceiling . . . he could not see well enough in the gloom of the dark, airless cell to see the ceiling. Not that it would have made any difference. Trussed like he was, he was not going anywhere, not on his own.

Weary from the effort of sitting upright and examining the very small world around him, Sam lay back down and closed his eyes. He needed to rest, he knew. He needed to regain his strength.

After a while the throbbing pain receded a little and he slept.

Sam woke the next time to the sound of a bolt being pulled open and the squeal of reluctant hinges. The cell was flooded with light when the door swung open. Two Mexican soldiers shouldered their way inside. The two bent and, each taking hold of him under his arms, lifted him onto his feet.

He had no strength in his legs. The soldiers held him up between them and dragged Sam out of the cell and down a short corridor to a large room where more soldiers were gathered. Two of those were guarding a raggedly dressed civilian who showed the bruises of a beating. The man was dark, with hair worn long and tied back with a headband Apache-style. He had distinctively Indian cheekbones. It was not possible to see what color his eyes were as they were swollen almost completely closed by the beating he had suffered.

Standing by a front window were the officer Sam remembered seeing earlier—Antonio the bartender had called him—and a slender, very handsomely dressed gentleman with sandy hair and a pencil mustache. The American said something to the lieutenant in Spanish, then crossed the room to closely inspect first the Indian prisoner and then Sam. He looked disappointed, but after a few moments grunted softly under his breath, then turned back and conferred with Antonio briefly.

The two of them seemed to reach some sort of agreement, although one that neither was completely happy with. The gent removed a coin purse from his coat pocket and selected a few yellow pieces that he gave to Antonio. The lieutenant clicked his heels and nodded briskly, then barked an order to his men.

Sam and the Indian were hauled outside and tossed, still in chains, into a steel cage that sat on the bed of a freight wagon pulled by a team of heavy draft horses. The cage door was closed and a padlock snapped shut to keep it that way.

"Take them out to the diggings, then come back here. I have some more work for you," the American said to whoever was on the driving box. Sam could not get a good look at the man with the reins. Not that it likely mattered. Not right now.

The only thing he was sure of at the moment was that he was in a pickle. Chained and presumably sold by the officer to this American civilian, although for what purpose he had been captured and for what reason sold, Sam did not yet know.

He suspected that he would not particularly like the answers when he got them, but for now those questions hardly mattered. Right now he needed to concentrate on recouping his strength. And regaining his freedom.

CHAPTER 7

Matt Bodine followed the wagon road around a curve and broke out over a wide bench on a hillside. Below it lay brown miles of rough, rolling countryside, above it a string of low mountains with dark foliage spotting the slopes and filling in the niches. Cattle grazed in the distance. On the bench itself was an adobe house, a log barn, a grouping of smaller outbuildings, and a set of corrals.

A thin stream trickling down from the mountain above fed a stock pond before running off down toward the flats, and Matt could see the stub of a water sump uphill from the house with pipe feeding into the back of the house. Now that was a mighty convenient touch, he thought. Water flowing fresh and clean right there inside the house. What would they think of next? But where did it go after it got inside? He could not see any outflow below the house. Surely the water had to go somewhere.

Matt kneed his horse into reluctant motion. The animal was not a good one, but he had swapped mounts twice on the way here, each time managing to get something a little better. This one was the best he'd been able to come up with, but he guessed he was at least a day and a half behind Sam.

Not that it mattered now. He was here and that was what counted.

Matt rode into the yard of Peter Branvol's Bar PB and drew rein in front of the house.

"Hello. Is anyone home? Hello in there." He remained in the saddle until a slender, very pretty Mexican woman in an apron and with her sleeves rolled up came in response to his call.

"Sí, señor?"

Matt swept his hat off and flashed his most charming smile. This was a very pretty woman indeed. And about his own age. "D'you speak English, miss? I'm looking for a Mr. Branvol. This is his place, isn't it?"

"Yes, I speak English. And yes, this is his place. Peter is not here at the moment but I . . . I expect him very soon."

"Then perhaps I could water this horse, miss, and wait for Pete."

"You may water your animal, sir. The trough is over there. It would not be proper for you to remain here without the presence of my husband, though."

"Your husband, ma'am?"

"I am Señora Branvol." She lifted her chin a little when she said it. Proudly. But defiant too. Matt could not help but wonder about that.

"You're Pete's missus?" Matt's smile was huge. "I'm awful pleased to meet you, ma'am. My name is Matt Bodine, and if you don't mind I'd like you to tell me where I can find Pete and my brother Sam."

"Peter is not here and . . . you say you have a brother named Sam?"

"That's right, ma'am. Pete sent a letter asking the two of us to come here. He didn't say why exactly, but he said he needed help. Where is he anyhow? And Sam? Where'd my brother get to?"

"I have never met this brother of yours, Señor . . .

Bodine, I believe you said? I do not know any Sam Bodine. And I cannot tell you where my husband is."

"Sam's last name is Two-Wolves, ma'am. We're actually blood brothers, not birth brothers, and . . ."

The woman's eyes went wide. "Blood brothers! From Wyoming in the United States, yes? Peter did mention you. He said . . . he said you would help us. Now . . . it may be too late for you to help."

"I don't understand," Matt admitted.

"My husband disappeared six days ago, Mr. Bodine. He rode out that morning like he always does. He did not come home that night."

"And you say you don't know Sam?"

"That is correct, yes."

"Sam should've been ahead of me maybe as much as two days, ma'am. I was sure I'd find him already here."

The pretty woman shook her head. "No, I have not seen him. I am sorry."

"I don't like the sound of any o' this, ma'am. Look, can I step down from this saddle and see to the horse? We've come a long way and he's nigh wore out."

"Excuse me, please. Where are my manners. There is a little grain in the barn. Give him that. Then come back here. You must be hungry too."

"I don't want t' put you out, Miz Branvol. . . ."

"My name is Anita, Mr. Bodine."

Matt bobbed his head in acknowledgment of the introduction, then continued. "Don't mean to put you to any trouble, but I do want t' ask you about the trouble Pete needs our help with." He turned and looked away toward the road he had just followed down from San Iba. "I sure would like to know what's become of Sam, though. I have a bad feeling about him. About Pete too."

, "Take care of the horse, Mr. Bodine. I will have food ready when you are done with him. We will talk then."

CHAPTER 8

It was a marvel, that's what it was. Just like Sam said they had back East. Pete had fixed up the outflow pipe from his spring box with a brass screw-valve sort of thing. When you wanted water, all you had to do was turn the handle and open that valve. When you were done, you turned it back the other way to stop the water from flowing. No wonder he hadn't seen any outflow from the house. There was even a collector-pipe sort of thing built into the bottom of a sump so the water would flow out if you wanted it to, like when you were done with it. Anita wouldn't even have to carry her used dishwater outside when she was done. She could just unplug that pipe and the water would run out to . . . somewhere. Matt hadn't figured that out yet.

He stood at the sink and turned the water on and then off again probably a half-dozen times before he was satisfied that he understood what Pete had worked out here. Anita stood aside and watched him with a small smile. She probably had seen this sort of reaction from visitors a good many times before.

Lunch was tortillas and spicy refried beans Mexican-style. There was no meat. Matt suspected the Branvols could not afford the luxury of butchering their own beeves, and there were neither pigs nor chickens on the place. The household garden, watered by the same creek that came down close by the house, produced mostly corn, beans, and peppers and was the likely source of the food Anita served now.

"This is good, ma'am, thanks."

"It is not too hot for you?" She smiled. "It is all right to tell me if so. I understand that you Americans have not the stomach of us peons."

"It's fine, ma'am. You say you haven't seen or heard from my brother Sam and you don't know what's happened to Pete either?"

The pretty young wife shook her head. "No, Señor Bodine. I wish I could tell you but I do not know."

"I'll be looking for the both of them then. Could you tell me, though, what trouble you and Pete are havin' here? Could you tell me why he wrote saying he needed help?"

"There is a man," Anita said. "An *americano*. He has taken a dislike to my husband. I do not know why he would do this."

"Me neither, ma'am. I admit it's been a while since either me or Sam saw Pete, but when we knew him he was an awful likeable fella. Easygoin' and always with a smile."

Anita gave a shy smile of her own, which caused dimples to appear on either side of her mouth. "He still smiles, my wonderful husband. His smile was what I first noticed about him. He made my heart full then. He still does."

Pete was a mighty lucky fellow, Matt thought. Mighty lucky indeed. But. . . . "Tell me about this man. You don't know what it is between him and Pete?"

"No, not really. Peter . . . I think he does not want to

worry me." Anita laid a hand flat on the front of her apron and her smile this time was positively beatific. "We will be blessed with a little one, God willing," she said.

"You're . . ."

She nodded happily. Then sobered again. "Peter worries about my condition. As if it was like an illness. You know?"

"That's kinda the American way," Matt said. "With us menfolk anyway. Women seem t' take to the notion easier than their husbands do."

"That is true on this side of the border too," Anita said. "Perhaps that is why Peter has not wanted to say much about our troubles."

"But this man, what can you tell me about him?"

"He owns much land to the north and the west. He owns many hectares."

"He raises cattle?"

She shrugged. "Who knows what he does. But he is a great friend of the governor of this state and of the military commander over the district. I know this to be true because before he came we were wanted here. Our business was desired. Not so now. Since this man came we have no friends in San Iba. The stores do not really wish to trade with us. They will sell us things, but for cash only. There is no credit while waiting for the calf crop to be sold. You know what I am saying? Do they have credit on the north of the border?"

Matt nodded. "You bet they do. It's the usual way of getting along. Folks got to live while they're waiting for money t' come in. Then when they sell their beeves, they go right away an' pay off whatever they owe and set aside what they have left over t' get them through the winter. Most of the time that ain't quite enough to carry them, so they got to run a tab again. Just the same as here."

"This man, I think he wants to make us leave. Peter has not told me this, but I believe it."

"What's this man's name, ma'am?"

"Please call me Anita. You make me sound so old."

"I'll try. Anita. Now who is this American who doesn't like Pete?"

"His name is Jarold Williams. Do you know of him?"

"No, I've never heard of him. But I guess I'll find out what I can."

"There is something you should know," Anita said.

"I'm listenin'."

"Three times, it could be more, Peter was troubled when he returned home. He did not say what was wrong. But he never used to carry a gun before this Williams came here. After the second time that Peter was so worried, he found his revolver in the chest where he had placed it out of sight. He cleaned it and loaded it and began to carry it with him whenever he rode away from the house, just to go down to the birthing pasture even. He never told me why he did this. But I am his wife. I knew that he was troubled."

Matt sighed. "We'll try an' get to the bottom of it," he said.

To himself he added, And I'll be tryin' to find out what's happened to Sam too.

Horse trouble, he hoped. Nothing more serious than more horse trouble.

Matt sure did wish the two of them hadn't gotten split up like this, though. He was worried. About Pete, but about Sam as well.

He dug into what remained of his dinner, wanting to surround it in a hurry so he could get about the business of trying to unravel this knot with Pete and Sam and a man named Jarold Williams.

CHAPTER 9

"The diggings," that fellow back in town had said. Sam understood what he meant now. The term was a description as well as a place. The diggings was a mine. A deep, open pit mine gouged out of solid rock. It was being dug deeper and rock extracted by seven men.

Just seven, Sam noted. Considering the size of the pit and the amount of work to be done, there should have been several times that number of miners doing the digging. Yet there were only seven.

Sam gathered that he and his companion in the prison wagon were intended to be the eighth and ninth miners in this hot and airless hole.

The seven who were down there were chained, although not with the manacles and leg irons that Sam wore now. The miners wore balls and chains, single ankle rings attached to four feet or so of chain with an iron ball at the end of it. The balls, which looked like solid shot for a cannon, were roughly a foot in diameter and must have been terribly heavy.

The miners could move almost freely within the limits of their chains, but if they wanted to go more than a pace or two beyond that, they had to pick the balls up and carry them with them, cupping both hands together and nestling the balls against their bellies, the weight of the metal making their movement more of a waddle than a walk.

Six of the men were attacking the rock with large, picklike tools heavy enough to shatter the stone into shards and splinters. They needed their hands free for the work, Sam saw, and needed to brace their feet wide apart in order to maintain their balance. That would account for the balls and chains. If they were chained like Sam was now, they would not be able to work in the pit.

The seventh was engaged in collecting the broken scraps of stone produced by the other six. That man had a wheelbarrow. He carried his iron ball in it along with the ore of whatever sort they were extracting here.

Sam watched as he took the wheelbarrow across the jagged, lumpy floor of the pit to a station against the wall, where he transferred the rock chips into an iron bucket at the bottom of a chain hoist that would lift the ore to the surface whenever the overseers wished.

There were three overseers visible, none of them actually down inside the pit. Two of the men, both of whom were white Americans, were armed with revolvers and shotguns. The third carried only a rod or cane no thicker than a man's little finger, a thin and whippy and rather ineffectual-looking thing that this one—a tall and very rugged-looking individual—swished back and forth through the air.

It was this man, who obviously was in charge, who came to meet the prison wagon.

"Two more, eh. Good. It's about time we got replacements for those we lost this past month," the overseer grumbled to the man—Sam still had not gotten a look at him—who was driving the wagon. The overseer, he noticed, was white but probably not an American. He had an accent that was almost but not quite British. "Just two? We could use a dozen. Two dozen."

"If you do not want the two, tell me."

"No, I want them, all right. Give me the key."

The overseer motioned for one of the shotgun guards to join him, then came to the rear of the wagon. He unlocked the cage and beckoned for Sam and the other man to come out.

Sam was acutely conscious of the shackles that weighed him down and severely restricted his movement. But he suspected the relative freedom of a single chain with an iron ball at the other end of it would be no improvement over what he suffered now.

He crawled slowly out of the cage. He had to turn and back carefully down to the ground like an infant just learning to go down stair steps. It was humiliating in addition to the physical annoyance. Finally, however, he did manage to stand clear of the wagon. He waited there while the Indian who had been his unspeaking companion for the hours-long journey crawled out too.

The man with the cane—it was made of bamboo, Sam could see when he got closer—waited until they were both out, then motioned for the driver to pull away, which he quickly did. Then the overseer turned to the chained prisoners.

"Do you understand English? Nod if you know what I am saying."

Sam nodded. The Indian beside him did not.

"You." The overseer pointed to Sam. "You say you speak English, do ye?"

Sam nodded again.

"Good. You." He pointed to the Indian. "Turn around

an' present your back." The Indian did not move or give any indication of understanding the instruction.

The overseer's lips thinned in what may have been intended as a smile. "We shall see, laddy, we shall see." He looked at the guard. "Turn 'im around, Bobby."

The guard motioned for the Indian to turn, and the man immediately faced away from the overseer.

"Down," the overseer snapped. When the Indian stood unmoving, the guard stepped closer and using the barrel of his shotgun, whacked the back of the Indian's knees, buckling his legs. Bobby moved closer and shoved, driving the chained man to his knees. Then Bobby pushed on the back of the Indian's head until he was bowed low and facing away from the overseer.

"Listen close to me, laddy. I'll be doing something now that ye'll not like even a little, but I shall stop—this one time will I stop—if only you ask me to. D'you understand? All ya need to do to make me stop is to say the word and there'll be no more. D'you understand that, eh?"

The Indian was motionless.

"I told you fair now, di'n't I?"

The bamboo cane flashed in the overseer's hand. The ends moved slightly apart when it passed through the air. Sam had not noticed that the cane was split until the overseer struck with it. The cane, or flail he supposed it might be called, whirred with all the vicious threat of a hornet's attack. When the flail landed on the Indian's back the impact had a sharp, surprisingly light sound. But the Indian stiffened and cried out aloud.

"Just say the word, laddy, when you want me t' stop," the overseer said.

The flail whirred again and again landed with little sound. But the back of the Indian's shirt split open under the sharp impact and there were already bright red welts rising where the bamboo struck.

"Stop. Please stop," the Indian cried out.

The overseer winked at Bobby and with a chuckle said, "Surprising, innit, how many o' them learn the King's English so suddenlike." He paused and added, "All right, lad. We've both proved our point. You can turn around an' stand up now."

When the Indian was on his own feet again, the overseer announced, "My name is Case Wilhelm. Boss Wilhelm to the likes of you. You can call me that or 'boss' or 'sir.' Call me anything else and you'll feel the cut of my lovely flail. Step out of line in any way an' you shall feel its sting. In a minute you will be fitted with your ankle chain and a wee anchor. The only way that chain will come off once it's on is to cut your foot off." His smile was cruel. "But any time you want the chain off, you just let me know. I will personally remove it for you.

"You're here to do a job. That's all. Just a job. Your sentence is eighteen months. I will write down in the book the date of your arrival. Eighteen months from now exactly you will be given a lunch and a dollar and set free. Until then you will perform hard labor. Very hard. No doubt about it. Very hard labor. And you will not like it. That is too bad, but you have no choice. You will serve every day of yer lawful sentence, make no mistake.

"If you cause trouble you will be caned. Try any run and the guards have authority to shoot. Think about that before ye try anything. Now . . . now I want youse to go with Bobby here. He will take you to the smithy. When you have your ankle chains, he'll show youse how to get into the pit where you'll be given tools an' start t' work off yer sentences.

"An' from this moment on, I will tolerate no complaints. Take what you are given. Give back an honest effort an' we'll have no problems, you an' me. But woe on ye if youse cause me trouble or torment, for I promise that I can give back more than you want t' bear. Now follow Bobby there to the smithy."

Wilhelm turned away, then stopped and spun back to face them. The evil, mirthless grin flashed again. "One thing I forgot t' mention. Whenever I walk near, you turn away and drop to your knees. Every time. *Every* time."

Wilhelm marched away, back stiff and shoulders squared. He looked . . . Sam was fairly sure of it . . . Wilhelm looked like a military officer out of uniform.

Sam glanced back into the pit where the seven prisoners continued to labor without any outward show of curiosity, although they surely had to know that there were newcomers up above them at ground level.

"Come along now. No lollygagging," Bobby ordered. "This way."

Sam and the Indian shuffled along, clanking and rattling, as fast as they were able.

CHAPTER 10

It took time to build and properly heat a charcoal fire for the forge, largely because Bobby might have been fine as a guard, but the man was no hand when it came to making a fire. He tried to start the bed of coals without using the bellows. Sam observed but did not offer to help him heat the rivets. He was in no dang hurry to have a ball and chain attached to his ankle.

By the time Sam and the Indian were securely fitted with their restraints, it was nearly dusk and too late for them to go down into the pit.

"Grab up those anchors and follow me," Bobby ordered. "Quick now."

Quick, the man said? They were not going anywhere quickly Sam realized the first time he bent and retrieved the ball. He was not sure what the solid iron sphere weighed, but his best guess would be in the neighborhood of forty pounds more or less. Light enough to drag or to carry. Heavy enough to severely hamper movement, especially when the four-foot-long chain was part of the problem.

Things would have been much easier had the chain

been just a foot or two longer, long enough to reach chest high or a little more so he could carry the ball on or over his shoulder. But of course there was a reason why the chain was not long enough for a man to do that, for it would make movement easier. And the whole idea of the ball and chain was to inhibit rapid movement—running away, for instance—without curtailing slow and deliberate motion.

Sam found that he could pick the ball up by the chain and carry it in one hand, but it was much easier to carry it in both hands cradled against his belly, exactly the way he already observed the other prisoners doing down in the pit.

Sam and the Indian waddled after Bobby to what looked like a root or storage cellar that had been dug into a solid rock hillside. A heavy door closed off the front. The door was wood, Sam noted, already thinking of escape. But it was secured by four thick iron bars that could be put in place to stop anyone from opening it.

At least, he saw when they stepped inside, they did not have to worry about being trapped by fire. The prison chamber was five feet wide and six high and ran too deep into the hillside for light to penetrate. Sam guessed it was an abandoned mine tunnel. No, dang it, that was not the correct word. He had to search his memory for a moment to come up with the right term. An adit, that was it. An adit runs into the ground; a tunnel runs all the way through and emerges on the other side. Sam wondered if this might indeed be a tunnel, if there might be an "other side" to find and escape through.

Pallets consisting of lumpy mattress tickings and ragged blankets showed this to be the living quarters of the captive laborers. A pair of oak buckets set near the doorway were provided for personal needs. There were no other furnishings, no lamps or candles. And no sign of personal possessions either, he noticed. No spare clothing. No books or combs or razors.

Bobby pushed them inside, then swung the door closed behind them with a thump. A moment later Sam could hear a bar being dropped into place to secure the door. Only one bar, though, he noticed. Bobby trusted them to stay put. Or possibly the guard knew something that Sam and his Indio companion did not.

The only light inside the adit now was the little that seeped in around the edges of the door. There was no window in it and no source of light deeper inside the mountain, at least none that could be seen from the entrance.

Sam grunted and closed his eyes, standing rigid with the iron ball against his belly completely forgotten. He raised his face toward the unseen sky and began to breathe the unspoken words of an ancient chant.

Strength was what he summoned from his ancestors and from the spirits of these foreign mountains. Strength and patience. Sam suspected he would be needing both of those.

When he opened his eyes again he felt light-headed but calm. He grunted again and took a step forward, the movement causing him to remember the ball in his hands. It suddenly felt impossibly heavy, and he set it down beside his right foot.

"You all right now?" a voice asked from the darkness ahead.

Sam blinked. He had to look carefully in the gloom to see that the speaker was the Indian who had traveled here with him from San Iba. Sam shivered, throwing off the last vestiges of the trance he had gone into, and nodded. "Fine, thanks."

"You were gone very long time," the Indian observed.

Sam smiled. "I intend to be gone much longer than that starting at the first opportunity."

The Indian grunted. "What language you pray in, brother?"

"Cheyenne."

"I am Yaqui."

"I have heard of your people. You are warriors."

"The Yaqui have heard of the Cheyenne too."

Sam introduced himself.

"I am Blue Runner. I am of the Snake clan, Two Wolf. I never know a Cheyenne warrior until now."

"Perhaps we will have a chance to fight side by side, Blue Runner. Perhaps we will do this when my brother comes to get me."

"You have a brother? Here?"

"Close by. Somewhere close by, Blue Runner. I can feel his presence."

"He will come?"

"He is my brother," Sam said. "He will come. As surely as I would come for him, friend, he will come."

Blue Runner's smile flashed white in the gloom. "Good."

CHAPTER 11

Matt borrowed the use of one of Pete Branvol's horses and saddled it, leaving his own weary nag in the corral. Pete's sorrel was young and fractious, but it was a pretty thing. Matt always had a weakness for beauty, in horses as well as in women.

The sorrel was an honest creature. It waited until Matt was firmly seated before it blew up. It snorted once, and exploded in all directions at once. At least that was what it felt like.

Matt's head flopped and wobbled like a chicken with a broken wing, and his spine felt like it was being played like an accordion; shoved down short whenever the sorrel's hoofs pounded into the ground, stretched almost to breaking every time it reached the top of a jump and started down again while Matt was still going up.

The horse could likely buck a tick off its back, or anyway thought it could. It did its level best to unseat Matt. He had to cling tight with everything he had. If he could've gotten a mouthful of mane between his teeth, he would have hung on with them too. Even if that interfered with the grin on his face. He was thoroughly enjoying the contest.

The sorrel worked him over for what seemed a terrible amount of time, but probably was no more than a minute or two to anyone who might have been a dispassionate observer.

Like the kid that was standing in the house doorway, hair tousled and eyes full of sleep. Matt recalled then that Pete's letter had mentioned a son. Probably the kid had been down for a nap when Matt got there. The boy looked to be three or maybe four. And he was certainly enjoying the show that Matt and the sorrel put on for him.

Matt rode the horse down to an agreeable settlement, then waved to the kid, who got bug-eyed and shy once he was caught watching. The child darted out of sight. Matt laughed.

The horse settled onto all four feet, shook itself like a dog coming out of water, and bobbed its head. Matt lightly squeezed with his knees and the sorrel stepped out in as pretty a road gait as he'd ever ridden. Fine horse, he thought. He wondered if Pete would be willing to sell it.

But first he had to *find* Pete. And Sam.

Wherever Sam was, whatever had happened, Sam surely knew that Matt would be coming to find him.

Matt took the sorrel down off the bench to a cattail-rimmed pond that was fed by the stream that passed by the house. A number of beeves bearing the Bar PB brand were lying in some scant shade nearby, looking for relief from the late afternoon heat.

If a man lived in this country, Matt thought, he would surely want to hang up his Stetson in favor of a straw hat that would let a little air reach his scalp. Lordy but it was hot down here.

Matt choused the cattle away from their shade, dismounted, and tied the sorrel to one of the three scrawny, thorny, twenty-foot-tall mesquites where the beeves had been. Manure, long since dried and scattered by trampling, showed that this was far from being the first time a horse had been tied here. No surprise, of course. Pete likely did the same often enough. And there was no way for Matt to read anything more than that into the fact, never mind that a host of Pete's enemies could have waited here for the young rancher to come down off the bench to check on his cattle.

Even so, Matt walked over to the pond and carefully inspected the ground close to the water where hoof- or footprints might have been left.

The ground was thoroughly churned by prints, but none was helpful. Cattle made most of the tracks. So did a good many birds of various sizes, one raccoon or something very similar to one, coyotes, and either a very large lynx or a rather small mountain lion. There were no horse prints at all and no footprints left by boots.

Matt checked both sides of the pond and both banks of the creek above the pond and along the very small outflow. The creek fizzled out and disappeared underground about a hundred paces below the pond, leaving a narrow wash below that point, the wash scoured out by heavy runoff in the rare wet years.

He walked back to the mesquites and reclaimed the sorrel—it offered no protest this time when he mounted—and rode it through the wash for a quarter mile until that intersected with a much larger gully.

He found a few prints here and there, but they indicated only one horse and thus very likely were Pete's tracks, left while he was working his own cattle, and not by someone who intended to waylay him.

Matt scrambled out of the wash onto the flat above using one of the many trails created by wild game or by cattle.

It was late in the day and he was no closer to knowing Pete's whereabouts—or Sam's—than when he arrived.

Still, he had to look close to the ranch before he went larruping off in other directions.

And come to think of it, he remembered now, he hadn't thought to ask Anita Branvol if Pete's horse came back home without him the day Pete disappeared. Matt turned the sorrel around and headed back to the ranch.

"Yes, it did," Anita said when Matt posed the question about the horse. "But it returned three days later and in its mane there were burrs of a kind that do not grow here."

The boy, his name was Ricardo in honor of Anita's father, stood huddled close to his mama's side with a thumb stuffed into the corner of his mouth.

Matt's eyebrows went up. "Are you sure . . . ?"

"Señor Bodine, I am not the fool. And I grew up on a small farm. I know my father's land and what grows there. I know this land and what grows here. I myself searched carefully for my Peter. I listened for his cries for help or for the sound of coyotes saying they found food. I watched the sky for the sight of vultures gathering. And until it returned, I looked for his horse. It was nowhere on our land or close to it.

"When the horse did come back, I looked at it carefully before I groomed it and put it into the corral. This horse, it was the same that you chose to ride today. When I found it standing outside the corral close by to the feed trough, it had burrs in its mane and a few in its tail, and there was dried mud above the hocks. This mud was gray, not the black mud of a meadow nor the yellow mud you see sometimes when there is wetness on the land below here, on our land. The gray mud . . . I think it must come from a mountain, Señor Bodine."

Matt turned to look toward the mountain that loomed above the Branvol homestead.

"No, not there, Señor. Peter would not go there. It is not our land, and there is a . . . a cluff you would say? An escarpment?"

"Cliff," Matt corrected.

"Oh, yes. Cliff. Thank you. My English, it is so—"

"It's fine. Really. What about this cliff?"

"It is steep. Cows, even sheep, have no way to climb it. So Peter never needs to worry about our livestock straying in this direction. He would have no need to be there and no trail to use without traveling far around."

"Yet the sorrel had gray mud dried on its legs," Matt mused aloud.

"Yes, Señor. This must have come from a mountain. Maybe this one." She shrugged. "Maybe another. I could not say. But to reach this mountain behind this place, one must travel many miles to either side in order to go around the cliff."

Matt sighed. "I think . . . I think tomorrow I'll ride back to San Iba. Maybe somebody's seen or heard something about Pete or about my brother. Surely somebody must know something."

"Perhaps," Anita said. She did not sound very hopeful. After a moment she smiled and ruffled Ricardo's curly hair. "Come. You can help me set the table for our supper, eh? You will excuse us, Señor Bodine?"

Matt nodded without really hearing what the woman said. His thoughts were elsewhere.

CHAPTER 12

Matt had to tilt his hat low to keep the sun out of his eyes as he rode into San Iba from the west. He had gotten an early start, not waiting for Anita Branvol and the boy to wake up. Between his worry about Sam and his concern for Pete, he hadn't been able to sleep anyway, so he'd figured he might as well put that predawn time to some use. He'd saddled his own horse, rested and road-ready now, and headed out in the dark in order to get here early.

The first order of business, Matt thought, would be to find a bite of breakfast. The rumbling and grumbling in his belly was telling him it was past time for that.

Matt drew rein in the middle of the street—there was not enough traffic in the sleepy town for that to cause any obstruction—and surveyed the possibilities. A hotel called the Cattleman's Inn looked promising. There was an outdoor patio with tables that suggested they provided meals for their guests, and a big breakfast was just what he needed.

Besides, it would give him an opportunity to start asking about Sam.

He dismounted and led the horse to a public water trough, gave it a moment to drink, and then tied it to a streetside hitch rail before walking back to the hotel.

The man behind the counter smiled and nodded when Matt came in. "Mornin', friend. What can I do for you?"

"Do you serve meals here?"

"Meals, rooms, liquor, pretty much anything a man needs," the proprietor responded.

Matt crossed the lobby to offer a smile and a handshake. He said hello and added, "I'm hungry as a bear in springtime, mister. Trot out two of everything on the menu, please."

The fellow chuckled and turned his head to call out something in Spanish, then returned his attention to Matt. "The boy will have it out quick as it's ready."

"Thanks. There's something else I'd like to ask while I'm waiting for the food."

"Sure. Ask anything you like. I'll either tell you God's honest truth or a really good lie."

"I'm looking for my brother. He should have come through here a few days ago. I don't know if he would have stayed the night, but if I know Sam he would've been powerful hungry by the time he got down here. He's about the same height as me, even looks a fair amount like me except he's got black hair and eyes and a darker complexion."

"Your brother, you say?" The man paused for a moment in thought. "No, sir, I don't recall anyone like that. We don't get so awful many strangers here, white men in particular. I'd remember for certain sure if I saw him."

"Thanks for trying to help. It was worth asking. Could I trouble you with one more question?"

"No trouble at all, friend. Go ahead."

"Me and my brother are down here to see an old friend. I believe you might know him. Pete Branvol."

"Of course I know Pete. He's a good man. Good neighbor. Are you needing directions to his place? I've never been there myself, but Doc Tippett ought to be able to help you. Doc isn't a regular doctor, you understand. He doctors horses. Owns the livery stable down at the other end of town. I expect he'd know."

"Oh, I know where to find the ranch. But Pete isn't there. Hasn't been for the past week or so."

The innkeeper shrugged. "I don't know as I can help you about that then. I haven't seen Pete in, oh, three or four weeks, I'd guess. Could be longer. He doesn't come in to town except every now and then. You know how that is."

"Yes, sir, I do. And I thank you for your help."

A slender Mexican boy of fifteen or so came out of the back carrying a wide, heavily laden tray. The aromas coming off the plates on that tray were good enough to get Matt's saliva flowing and his stomach rumbling again.

"You'd best pick a table and set down if you want that breakfast, friend," the innkeeper said.

Matt was quick to take the man's advice.

When he was done eating—it took a while as there was a mountain of food there and he was determined to get around as much of it as he could—Matt went next door to a pleasant little saloon. He figured there wasn't so much to San Iba; he could walk both sides of the business district asking for Sam and for Pete. Surely someone here must have seen Sam, even if he had only ridden through the town without stopping.

Sam could have met someone on the road who gave him directions to the Bar PB. He did not absolutely have to have stopped in San Iba. But he certainly had to ride through the town.

If, in fact, he got this far.

Something could have happened to him before he ever arrived in the vicinity.

Matt's stomach lurched and he felt a chill run up his spine at that thought.

Sam might have been waylaid on the road. Between here and the border. Up in Arizona somewhere. Anyplace. Still. . . .

Matt shook his head and scowled. No. If Sam for some reason was ambushed and murdered, Matt would know it. The connection between them was strong enough that Matt surely would feel it if Sam were killed. The bond between the blood brothers ran deep.

Sam Two-Wolves was *not* dead. Matt knew that in his bones.

But Sam was in trouble. Matt could feel that too. Wherever Sam was, it was cause for worry.

If he had to talk to every man, woman, and child in San Iba in his search for Sam, well, that was what he would do.

Starting with this quiet saloon.

CHAPTER 13

All seven of the prisoners let into the cavelike cell were Indians. No white men, Sam noticed, and no Mexicans either. Four of the men were Yaquis. They already knew Blue Runner and immediately drew him off and began conversing in their own language. The other three were Apache, two of whom spoke English.

"What is it like here?" Sam asked a middle-aged Apache man called Nana. The others were Koronado and Tomas. Koronado spoke a little English.

All nine men squatted close to the entrance, Sam and Blue Runner because that was where they happened to be standing when the others were brought in, the seven experienced prisoners as if they were waiting for something.

"It is bad," Nana told him. "Hard. Dig, dig, more dig. Boss man want the stone."

"Do you know why? What kind of ore it is?"

Nana shrugged. "Who knows, eh? Crazy in the head, these whites."

They were interrupted by the sound of bolts being drawn and the creak of hinges opening. It was dark outside, but the night was far brighter than the inside of the cell, bright enough for Sam to see Wilhelm and a guard standing by with shotguns while another guard brought in buckets that had been delivered on a hand-drawn wagon. There were nine of the galvanized steel buckets. One by one the prisoners each retrieved a bucket until two were left.

The Yaquis said something and Blue Runner too took a bucket. Nana motioned for Sam to pick up the last. It was heavy and there was a mighty good smell rising out of it.

"Eat," Koronado said. The massive door was pushed closed, blocking out all sight of the outside world and taking the light with it. Again there was the sound of bolts and now heavy bars as well.

"In morning," Sam could hear Nana in the darkness, "they bring more food. Give this pot. Exchange. You see?"

"Yes, I understand."

"Little time to eat, then go dig. Two meal each day. Only water in the pit. No food. No siesta. Just dig."

Sam tasted the rich stew. He had to scoop it with his fingers as there was no spoon provided. The stew was good and there was plenty of it. It was not hot, but at least it was acceptably warm. Sam quickly learned that the easiest way to eat the stew was to raise the bucket and drink the stew rather than trying to scoop it up. He used his fingers to drag the chunks of meat, rice, and carrot to the lip of the bucket so he could get to those. As his eyes became adjusted to the lack of light, he saw that the others were doing much the same, except for Blue Runner, who sat with his bucket in his lap and ate with his hands.

There was no provision for washing, at least none that Sam saw. He asked the Apaches.

"No," Koronado told him. "Rub dirt. No water."

Sam sighed. The accommodations here were not what a fellow might hope for.

"At least they feed well. They aren't trying to starve anyone," he observed.

"Must be strong," Nana said. "You need food to be strong so you can dig the stone for them."

Sam grunted. "I don't think I would like eighteen months of this though."

"Eighteen . . . ?"

"That's how long my sentence is, or so they said. A year and a half. And I don't even know why."

Nana repeated that in his own tongue and the Apaches all laughed.

"Did I say something funny?"

"Eighteen month? Brother, no one lives so long here. You will be dead long before that. Eight, ten month maybe so."

Tomas said something and Nana nodded, then translated for Sam. "There was a man once who live more than a year. That is what they say. But then they want you to believe this. Want you to believe you will live long enough to be set free. You will not. If you dig eighteen month but still live, they will not allow you to go anyway. No one leaves here except down the hill."

"Down the hill?" Sam repeated. "What hill? What is down it?"

Nana pointed toward the door and the free world beyond. "Down there, down the mountain, sometimes we turn the wheel. We break the stone. Grind it like corn on the metate. You know what I am saying?"

"Yes, I think so. Like grinding meal with a mill wheel."

"Yes. Arrastra grinds stone. We turn the wheel. Not so hard as to dig so it is good to have this job. The sick are allowed to work at the arrastra. What is left after they take what they want from this small stone and dust, whatever is left is thrown over the side. Thrown down the hill. When a man dies here, he too is thrown over the side there. Down the hill. Then soon the stone falls down. Covers him and he is seen no more. That is what I mean by 'down the hill,' Sam Two Wolf. To be down the hill is to be dead."

"Well, I don't know about you boys," Sam said, "but I intend to live and to walk out of here a free man. And I don't expect to take any eighteen months to do it."

"If you find a way, good. But I must tell you, Sam Two Wolf, we have looked for a way to leave. There is nothing."

Sam did not argue with the friendly Apache. But he did not agree with the man either. There *was* a way. He just did not yet know what it was.

But he would. He was determined that he would.

CHAPTER 14

Living as wanderers had hardened the blood brothers and inured them to the hardships of living outdoors. Sleeping on the ground was normal for both of them, so much so that they could be comfortable anywhere.

Or so Sam had believed until now.

He woke the following morning and got a second sort of wake-up when he sat upright. He hurt. Darn near everywhere. His hips and shoulders ached from sleeping on hard, bare rock with no blanket or sougan to act as a pad between flesh and stone. His back hurt. His elbows hurt. The back of his head hurt. His ankle especially hurt from the steel shackle that encircled it.

"Hey. Two Wolf."

Sam was surprised that he was able to see fairly clearly in the gloom now that his eyes were so thoroughly adjusted. He stifled a yawn—he certainly had not slept well—and said, "Good morning, Nana."

"Your foot, it is sore? There where the metal touches?"

"Yes, very much so."

"Be careful. If you pull too much it will tear and bleed. Can become . . . infected?"

"Yes, that's the word. Infected," Sam offered.

Nana nodded. "I have seen men's foots rot from the infected. They get the stinking flesh and then they die. Tear the bottom of your shirt. Push that between the metal and the meat. It will help."

"Thank you." Sam had just finished padding the shackle when he heard the iron bars and steel bolts being withdrawn at the door. The others picked up the food buckets they had been given the evening before, so Sam did the same.

The door swung open, admitting a rush of pale gray predawn light. One by one the men exchanged their empty buckets for full ones and quickly retreated back into the adit.

"Not long time," Koronado grunted. "They back soon."

Breakfast was another stew, rich with gravy and fats and plump grains of rice. The people here wanted their slaves to have strength.

That was something to consider, Sam mused as he ate. Whoever was doing this and for whatever purpose, they valued the slaves and wanted them to survive. The guards very likely would be reluctant to kill or disable.

And hesitation on their part might give a man valuable seconds of safety when it came time for him to make his break.

As soon as he figured out how to do that, that is.

He glanced down toward the heavy ball that was so firmly attached to his leg and frowned. He darn sure was not going to outrun anybody. Not while he was carrying that thing.

Koronado touched Sam lightly on the elbow to gain his attention. "Obey," he advised. "Always obey."

"Thank you for your concern, brother."

Koronado grunted.

The guards returned and the men picked up their steel balls and formed a line at the door. As soon as the door was pulled open, they filed outside into the young daylight. Blue Runner and Sam came out last. The guards herded them toward the lip of the pit, toward the start of a narrow path that angled down the wall of the dig.

The men in front stopped short, however, when Case Wilhelm appeared. The boss guard this time carried the thin flail instead of a shotgun. He wore a revolver on his hip.

As Wilhelm came near, the older men quickly dropped to their knees, heads down and eyes averted. Blue Runner hesitated, then did the same.

Sam looked at them, then at Wilhelm. The thought of kneeling to a bullying thug like this was abhorrent. His Cheyenne ancestry filled his chest with stubborn pride.

Sam Two-Wolves stood upright and proud while the others submissively knelt.

This, he realized, was what Koronado warned him about just a few moments earlier. Submit. Obey. Or suffer the consequences.

The overseer's eyes locked with Sam's, and for a moment the big man seemed almost pleased at this show of resistance. He glided nearer and his expression hardened.

"Down," he hissed. Wilhelm's voice was low, little more than a whisper.

Sam bent, but only to place the iron ball beside his feet. He stood upright again, back straight and chin held high. His eyes bored coldly into Wilhelm's.

"You will learn," Wilhelm said. "This I promise. You *will* learn." The overseer walked around behind Sam.

Sam heard a swish like that of an arrow's flight and a streak of pain exploded across his shoulders as the bamboo flail struck with a viper's vicious speed.

Sam steeled his nerves, determined he would not flinch, would not bend, would not kneel to this man.

He closed his eyes and retreated deep inside his head, his thoughts directed to the chants of his people as he asked for courage.

The beating continued, but after a while Sam no longer felt it. What he felt was Wyoming wind gentle on his face and the Wyoming sun warm on his brow. In his mind he rose up to meet an eagle in the air and soared with it as the great bird swept majestically above the vast, grassy plains. Sam thought he could see his grandfather's approving face and his father's smile.

It was good to see them again, Sam thought as he soared higher. It was good.

CHAPTER 15

San Iba might not be all that big, but it was hot and dry and dusty, and by the time Matt finished talking to every human person and a pair of small dogs he found at the cantina end of town, he was dry and dusty himself. He headed back to Tim Rogers at his saloon for a beer and a little shade before tackling the livery end of town.

Yessir, he was thinking as he got there, if he lived down here permanent, he would for certain sure want to trade his fine Stetson for a lightweight straw hat. He removed the Stetson and ran a hand through his hair as he entered the pleasant little saloon.

Rogers was behind the bar as he had been when Matt talked to him earlier. Now Tim was speaking with a tall, smiling gent who was leaning his elbows on the bar and huddling over a brandy snifter like he was protecting it. Not that he needed to, of course. There were three other customers nearby who were paying no attention whatsoever to Tim and his friend.

The clutch of three men standing belly-up to the bar were all rough-dressed and rough-looking. There was something about them that suggested they were muscle hired by someone here, or perhaps were down on this side of the border to evade the law back in the States.

One in particular appeared to fancy himself as a gunfighter. At least he dressed the part. He wore a flat-crowned brown hat, filthy yellow brocade vest, and knee-high mule-skinner boots that should have been put out to pasture years ago.

He wore two guns, each slung very low on his thighs with the holsters strapped down tight. It was a look meant to inspire fear. Matt thought it was silly.

And awfully impractical if the idiot ever got into a real-life gunfight.

Carrying those guns extra low like this man did was a telltale giveaway of his ignorance. Guns carried down there have to be held in the holster by some means, usually a thong looped over the spur of the hammer. If the weapon is not carefully contained, it can drop out onto the ground whenever its owner sits in a chair, takes his seat on a saddle, or especially when a horse he might be riding gets into a storm—in short, whenever his leg is in anything other than a straight up-and-down posture. The thong works well enough to avoid that, but when trouble is expected, the thong can be slipped off and pushed out of the way.

But then trouble does not always come when it is expected.

Matt frowned when he saw that this man did indeed use short bits of whang-leather thong to hold his guns in place. And right now those thongs had been tucked aside.

Of course it could simply be that he had the habit of carrying them like that until he decided to mount a horse or climb stairs or otherwise cause those holsters to leave the perpendicular.

It could be.

But then it could be that there would be a blizzard on the Fourth of July too. Matt did not believe that either.

He angled toward the other end of the bar. Tim excused himself from the smiling gent and turned toward Matt. "What will you have, friend?"

"Beer, I reckon. That's all I need, thanks."

"Did you find your brother or do any good looking for Pete?" Tim asked as he drew the foamy beer.

"Not yet," Matt admitted. He placed a nickel in U.S. money onto the bar and buried his nose in the suds. The beer cut through the dust in his throat and tasted mighty good.

When he looked up again he saw that the fellow who thought himself a gunfighter was ambling over toward him. "Did he say you're the fella that's looking for Pete Branvol?"

"That's right," Matt said.

The gunfighter stopped about three paces short of Matt and stood facing him instead of turning to the bar. "I might be able to help you," he said.

"I'd appreciate it if you could," Matt told him.

"I ran into Pete a few days ago. About, oh, I dunno. A week. Could be a little less."

"Yes?" Matt took another sip of his beer and set the mug back onto the bar. He turned and leaned his left elbow beside the mug, which had him more or less facing the gunfighter. He smiled. "Did Pete happen to say where he was going?"

"Matter of fact, mister, he did. He told me he was done with this country. Said he was tired of Mex lingo and runny-nose kids. Pete said he was pulling up stakes and drifting on. Said something about California or maybe going on up to Canada for a fresh start."

"Is that a fact?"

"Yes, it is. Pete's gone from this country. No need for you to look for him no more."

"Thanks for the information, but I expect I'll keep on looking for him."

"There's no need for that. I'm telling you he's pulled out. Gone. He left that little Mex tart and her half-breed kids."

Matt sighed. "Mister, I don't know why you want me to believe that, but it isn't working. I know that isn't the truth."

The man bristled and squared his shoulders, scowling menacingly. "Are you calling me a liar?"

"Not at all. You could simply be misinformed. You might have a very strange sense of humor and be trying to pull a practical joke on me." Matt smiled. "Of course, the possibility always exists that you could indeed be a liar. But I wouldn't know that, would I?"

The gunfighter growled. He gritted his teeth and actually growled out loud. Matt managed to avoid laughing.

"You'll take that back, mister, or you'll face me. And you'd best know one thing. I'm the fastest gun in this whole country."

Matt straightened to his full height. He checked the gunfighter's companions at the other end of the bar. They, Tim, and the pleasant-faced gent all shifted quietly aside to be out of the line of fire, but none of them appeared to be taking a hand in whatever this was.

Matt's lips thinned into a tight smile.

"Maybe you were the fastest," he said. "Until I got here."

CHAPTER 16

"Last chance, mister. Back water or die." He bent slightly at the waist and moved his feet a little farther apart so he was in a crouch, ready to sweep his guns out of their holsters. His fingers curled in anticipation of grabbing the butts of the revolvers. He looked to be strung so tight he would make a sound like a violin if someone ran a bowstring over him. This man was ready for a fight and then some. More than simply ready, he seemed positively eager for it.

Matt was unfazed. He stood normally, to all outward appearances relaxed. His hands hung calmly at his sides. "I think we have more choices than that, you and me," he said. "We don't have to drag iron here. We can talk about this." Matt smiled. "Or you can . . . how did you put it? You can back water. Which probably would be the sensible thing for you t' do."

The gunfighter sputtered. "M-me! You want me to back water? Why, for two cents I'd . . ." He blustered and babbled for a moment in incoherent rage, then stuttered to a halt.

"Two cents? I have that much in my pocket. You can

have it if you want. I'd rather you just turn and go an' leave me in peace to finish my beer and go on looking for my brother." Matt's voice turned hard. "But if you want those two pennies, mister, they're yours if you're man enough to take them. Fists, guns, knives, however you like it."

Matt truly hoped the man would walk away. He knew that was not possible, though. The fellow had made his brag and his threat where others could hear. Now he had to grab for his guns if only to show that he was not a coward.

It seemed a pity.

The gunfighter's expression twisted into a vicious
 . . . He had no thought of losing, it was clear; such a
 . . . ed his mind because he was, after all,
 . . . und. Or so he believed.
 . . . flashed with the speed of a striking
 . . . d fingers clawed at the grips of his re-
 . . . began to rise, the barrel pulling smoothly
 . . . ather while at the same time his thumb
 . . . mmer and began pulling it back.

The cylinder loaded with thick, stubby, deadly cartridges began to turn with the movement of the hammer, even while the weapon remained within the confines of the holster.

His eyes were locked on this stranger in front of him, the cheeky stranger who . . . Oh, God!

The gunfighter's eyes widened with shocked recognition as for one short instant he was aware that this man standing in front of him was freakishly fast.

He saw that Matt's Colt was already out, cocked, and leveled even before his gun could clear leather.

He saw a flash of bright yellow fire bloom at the muzzle of that Colt.

He felt a jolt. An impact. On his breastbone. He staggered half a step backward, caught and righted himself. Tried to remember what he was—

Oh, yes. His gun. He had to . . . had to take it out. Had to . . . he could no longer remember why he needed it, what he was supposed to do with it. But he knew he should take it out.

He tried. He had his hand wrapped tight around the smooth, familiar grips of his pistol. He lifted. Heavy. The gun was heavy. So terribly heavy that he could not . . . he could try. He pulled. Pulled hard.

He felt another impact. This one high on his chest. The force of it spun him around.

He could see the bar. The array of bottles behind it.

He was still turning. Why was he still turning around?

He could see Jim and Lawrence and Tim and Mr. Williams.

He could see . . . why, he could see the ceiling. Was that funny? All the dozens and dozens of times he'd in here and he'd never noticed the ceiling before.

It was hard to see it right now, though. It ting dark. My, he hadn't known it was so late. getting dark all right, though. He could barely see the face of . . . was that Lawrence? Whyever was he sideways instead of straight up and down? And the ceiling. Why . . .

Dark. Very dark now.

And cold.

From somewhere far away he heard howling. Coyotes? A huge pack of coyotes? Or . . . demons.

The howling was coming closer and the dark cold was closing over him.

* * *

Matt stood poised, waiting to see if anyone else wanted to mix into this. No one did. One of the men who had been with the gunfighter turned and ran out of the saloon. Tim the bartender and the other two men stood in stunned silence for a moment; then they came forward.

The rough-looking fellow who had been with the gunfighter dropped to his knees and peered down at his friend. The gunfighter's mouth opened and Matt thought he was going to speak, but the light of life in his eyes was snuffed out and the only thing to come out of his mouth was a trickle of blood that ran across his cheek and into his ear.

Matt wanted quite badly to eject the spent brass from his Colt and reload those chambers, but he did not want to do it while these others were there. For the moments it would take to reload, the Colt would be inoperative, and Matt did not want to find himself disarmed among these strangers.

"Sorry 'bout this," Matt said to the proprietor, Tim. "He didn't give me a choice."

Tim raised his voice and called out something in Spanish. A few moments later two boys came hurrying in. They took the gunfighter by the hands and dragged him outside. Along with them was a young woman, little more than a girl really, wearing a peasant blouse and a skirt that in Wyoming would have been scandalously short, but which here seemed to be normal attire. She brought sawdust and a broom and began cleaning up the blood. Matt got the impression this was not the first time blood had been spilled on this floor.

The pleasant gent who had been talking with Tim earlier stepped forward, and Matt got the idea he intended to say something, but he was interrupted by the arrival of a Mexican Army officer and two soldiers with bayonets mounted on their muskets.

Matt looked at the officer's expression, and definitely wished he'd had time to replace those expended cartridges in his Colt.

The officer started forward with a scowl, but the tall gent stopped him with a touch on the officer's sleeve. The two conversed for a moment in Spanish, the American's Spanish quite as fluid as the Mexican's; then the officer gave a command. The soldiers snapped to attention, saluted, and marched out the door and out of sight. The officer gave Matt a hard, speculative look; then he too turned and left.

The pleasant-faced gentleman came forward. "I didn't mean to intrude," he said, "but I took the liberty of clarifying to Lieutenant Espinosa that you fired only in self-defense."

"Thank you. I appreciate that."

The gent extended his hand. "I am Jarold Williams. I live here. And you would be . . . ?"

Matt gave his name and shook Williams's hand.

"I will not say that meeting you is a pleasure, Mr. Bodine. Not under the circumstances. But you clearly had no choice. Curly forced the issue."

"Curly," Matt repeated. "Did he have a last name?"

"Undoubtedly, but I never knew what it was. Perhaps one of his friends will know what to put on the marker."

"Yes. I, uh, I'll pay for the burying," Matt said.

"No need for that. I will pay," Williams said. "Curly worked for me, you see. Burying him is the least I can do."

"I see."

"Now that Curly is dead, Mr. Bodine, I have an opening for a man with your rather spectacular abilities. I would like to hire you, sir."

"That's kind of you, Mr. Williams, but I've already got my plate full looking to find Pete Branvol and hook up with my brother. He was supposed to meet me down here and he hasn't shown up yet."

"I see. Well, if you change your mind, Mr. Bodine, I'll not be hard to find. Come see me any time."

"Thank you, sir. Now if you will excuse me, I need to go see the man at the livery, see if maybe he knows something about my brother or Pete."

Williams smiled and turned away. Matt looked around. Tim was busy behind the bar and Curly's friends had left when the body was carried out. Matt stepped over to the bar and quickly reloaded his Colt.

After all, a man never knows.

CHAPTER 17

The spirit of Sam Two-Wolves returned to earth with fire and power. The fire was in his back, where it felt like it must surely consume his flesh to the bone. The power was in the corded muscles of his neck and jaw as he braced himself to keep from crying out aloud.

But that he would not do. He would not give them the satisfaction of hearing him moan lest they think he was begging for their mercy. As if these insects were capable of mercy. As if they even knew what it was. Sam ground his teeth together and concentrated on holding his silence. And bearing his pain.

"The white ones are gone," a voice in his ear whispered over and over. "You can return now. They are gone."

Sam shuddered and opened his eyes. He was back in the prison tunnel—no, not a tunnel, an adit, that was it—along with the others. He had not been aware of the passage of time, but it seemed to be night. Sam was lying facedown on a pallet of old rags. Nana was kneeling at his side along with Blue Runner and another of the Yaqui.

The silent Yaqui picked up a plump spear of succulent

cactus and used his thumbnail to split the cactus flesh, exposing a green ooze that he smeared onto Sam's back. The jellylike cactus was shockingly cold at first touch. Then it melted into the damaged skin. Soothing. Healing. The effect was immediate. It was not complete. There was still pain. But the worst of the fire had been extinguished.

Sam peered at the odd fat, thornless cactus leaves and raised an eyebrow.

"Aloe," Nana said. "It is one of the healing plants. They let us pick some today on our way back from work."

"Have I . . . have I . . . ?" It took Sam a moment to find his tongue. "How long?"

"Two days. They thought you would die. Old Man Leather Shirt say you will live." Nana grunted. "The white ones were wrong."

Old Man Leather Shirt—he did indeed have a leather shirt but he was far from being old—continued to apply the marvelously soothing aloe jelly, splitting one leaf after another and tossing the used ones aside.

"Tomorrow they will want to see you kneel."

"A man is free to want whatever his heart pleases, eh."

"You will kneel?"

Sam grimaced. "I will not."

Nana nodded and said something to the others. Old Man Leather Shirt cackled, a dry sound that it took Sam a moment to realize was laughter.

"Can you move?" Nana asked.

"I think so."

"Tomorrow you will be expected to work."

"That I can do. But I will not kneel to them."

"You will do what is right for you to do," Nana said.

"That I will," Sam said.

"Sit up now. Your supper is here."

"Thank you." Sam accepted their help, Nana's and Blue Runner's, to pull him upright. His head spun dizzily, but he shook it off and felt much better once he was sitting up.

Nana grinned. "We ate the food they gave for you yesterday and this morning."

Sam smiled ruefully and shrugged. Old Man Leather Shirt tossed the rest of the aloe aside and handed Sam a bucket of stew to rebuild his strength for tomorrow's trials.

In the morning there was no sign of Case Wilhelm when the prisoners were led out for their work assignments. Three of the other guards handled them.

"You." One of the guards gestured toward Sam with the muzzle of his shotgun. "Arrastra. And you." He pointed to Blue Runner.

"I told you they want us to live," Nana muttered just loudly enough for Sam to hear. "They need our work. Today you will have easy work. So you get strong again. Later you go to the pit. Today not so bad."

"Anything a man is required to do that involves him being in chains is bad," Sam said.

"Quiet!" a guard snapped.

Sam stood silent and glowering while the others were marched away to the pit while he and Blue Runner were left on the surface. One guard remained with them. He motioned with his shotgun and the prisoners started shuffling down a path to the bowl-shaped arrastra where they would be expected to turn a huge, wheel-like disk of stone to pulverize ore from the pit the same way grains of wheat are ground into flour by the miller's wheel.

The only halfway good thing about the task, aside from it being considerably less taxing than the backbreaking labor and ferocious heat inside the pit, was that lengths of chain were suspended from the thick wooden pole that ran through the stone like an axle. The prisoners were required to push on that pole, turning in circles round and round. The chain was there so they could hang their anchoring iron balls on the drive bar, freeing their legs of that drag while they made their slow, incessant circles around the arrastra.

The guard explained the process for the new men, miming the actions as well as giving verbal instruction so as to get through to them in case they did not speak English. Then he said, "All you do is keep that thing turning. An' don't think about stopping 'less I tell you so. I'll give you a break about noon so's you can have you some water. Other than that jus' do what you're told and we won't have no trouble, you'uns and me."

No trouble? Sam thought, looking at the guard. Little man, you have no idea.

But he said nothing and his expression gave no hint of the hatred that seethed deep in his belly.

Sam reached for the iron S-hook to clip his iron ball onto the axle bar, then stood as patient and outwardly docile as any donkey while Blue Runner went around to the other side of the crusher to take his position there.

When Blue Runner was ready the guard called out to them. "Begin."

Sam leaned into the bar and began to push.

CHAPTER 18

Matt stopped beside his horse, still tied outside the saloon, and unbuckled the near saddlebag. He reached inside for the yellow pasteboard box of cartridges there, and frowned a little when he realized how light it was. There were only—he counted—ten of the fat brass cartridges remaining. He stuffed those into empty loops on his gun belt and took the yellow box in one hand and the horse's reins in the other.

He wanted to make a stop at the hardware anyway and he might as well do it now, on his way to the livery where the bartender said he might get word about Sam. He tied the horse to a rail near the hardware and went inside the adobe-walled building, grateful for the shade and the relative coolness inside.

"Yes, sir, what can I do for you?" the proprietor asked.

Matt dropped his empty cartridge box on the counter and said, "I'd like a couple boxes of these, thank you, and some information if it suits you."

"The ca'tridges I got. The information I'll share if I have what you need." The fellow opened a cabinet beneath the counter, took out two very heavy little boxes, each holding fifty rounds of ammunition, and set them onto the counter with a thump. "Dollar fifty apiece for the ca'tridges. Now what information would you be wanting?"

Matt paid for his ammunition and inquired about Pete Branvol and Sam Two-Wolves.

"I know Pete, o' course. He's a good man. Haven't seen him in, oh, prob'ly a couple weeks, though. He didn't say anything about taking a trip or nothing like that. As for your brother"—the man shook his head—"I haven't seen anybody like that. I wish I could help you. Sorry."

Matt smiled and thanked him and started to turn away, then stopped again, his attention riveted on a half-dozen or so holstered revolvers hanging from a coat tree behind the counter.

"See something you like there, do you?" the store-keeper asked.

"I dunno. Maybe. That rig at the bottom. With the plain leather and brass buckle. Could I see that gun, please?"

The storekeeper obligingly took the gun belt down, pulled out the revolver, opened the loading gate, and turned the cylinder to assure himself that the gun was un-loaded and safe to handle, then passed it across to Matt.

Matt felt a chill run up his spine. This was Sam's .45. And Sam's holster as well. Lord knows Matt had seen gun and belt often enough to know them now.

"What d'you know about this gun?" he asked.

The storekeeper shrugged. "Not much. Bought it off Lieutenant Espinosa. He's the officer in charge of the garrison here. I don't know how he come by it. It isn't something he woulda been issued by the Mexican government, though, so I figure he wasn't selling government property or nothing like that. Tell you the truth, mister, I didn't need another used gun to sit around gathering dust, but it's a good idea to stay on the sunny side of that lieutenant. And he offered to sell it to me cheap. If you're interested, I'll pass it along for a good price."

"I'm interested," Matt said grimly, digging into his pocket for money to buy Sam's Colt back.

Five minutes later, Sam's gun belt rolled and tucked away in Matt's saddlebags, Matt led his horse into the livery barn. "I'm looking for a man named Doc Tippett," he said to the elderly fellow who emerged from the tack room blinking and rubbing at his eyes. Matt seemed to have roused him from a nap. "Tim Rogers down at the saloon said I might could find Tippett here."

"I'm Tippett. Got trouble with your horse?"

"No trouble, no, but I'd be willing to make a swap if you have anything I like."

"I have a few head out back that you can look over. Help yourself while I take a gander at your animal."

Matt nodded and passed through the barn and outside to a corral in back. There were five head of saddle stock in the pen along with a pair of long-eared mules and a burro.

One of those horses belonged to Sam Two-Wolves.

Matt's jaw clenched tight and he fought back an impulse to break into a rage.

He regained control by the time Tippett came outside to join him.

"See anything you like?"

"Yes." Matt jerked his chin in the direction of Sam's animal. "What can you tell me about that one?"

"I don't know much about him. My hired man's son took him in when I wasn't here. Said some Indio had him. Yaqui maybe, Apache, one of them. I wasn't here so I wouldn't know. Anyway, the Indian never came back. I asked the *alcalde* about it and he said I should consider the horse as abandoned property. He gave me a bill of sale to make sure everything was on the up and up."

"And this *alcalde* of San Iba?" Matt asked. "Who would he be?"

"Lieutenant Antonio Espinosa. He's the commander of the Army garrison in addition to his civil duties." Tippett spit. "Whatever they are."

"You don't care for the lieutenant?"

"No more'n I care for a basket full of rattlesnakes. In fact, somewhat less. But if you live in San Iba you take Espinosa along with the good."

"That horse belongs to my brother Sam."

"Espinosa said—"

"Sam's father was a respected chief of the Cheyenne nation, but his mother is a lady from a wealthy Boston merchant family."

"And he's your brother?"

"Blood brother," Matt said. "We grew up together."

"Mister, if I was you, I'd ride right on outa here and say nothing more about this. The lieutenant, he don't like to admit he could ever make a mistake."

"Well, he made a good one this time. What has happened to Sam? Is he in jail? What will Espinosa have done with him?"

"I don't actually know anything, mind you. I never been out there."

"There?"

"What I've heard is that Espinosa hires out convict labor to a white man named Jarold Williams."

"I've met Williams," Matt admitted.

"Williams is said to have a place out on Conquistador Mountain. But like I said, I never been there myself. All

I know is hearsay and you know what that can be worth."

"Tell me anyway."

"When he first come here, Williams tried to hire local labor to work out there. He wanted to reopen an old mine, he said. But the Mexicans and the local Indians won't have anything to do with Conquistador. They say that mountain is cursed. They say it's an evil place. If you just mention it out loud they'll start to pray and cross themselves to ward off the evil spirits. I've seen them do it. For whatever reason they are right serious about it. The place frightens them so bad Williams couldn't get a one of them to take his money. And I hear tell that what he wants done is work that no white man is gonna accept neither. So he pays Espinosa for convict labor."

"It sounds like a dirty game," Matt said.

"So it is, but it's common enough. Most any prison in this country hires out convicts for labor."

"I'll want to buy my brother's horse and rig off of you, Mr. Tippett. And I'm still interested in making a swap for my own use. Maybe for that ugly thing in the corner over there if he moves and rides all right." He pointed toward a bay standing hipshot and lazy behind the others.

Tippett snorted. "Ugly, yes, but he might be the best horse in this county barring your brother's animal. You have a good eye for horseflesh."

Tippett led the bay out and gave Matt time to inspect it. The horse was eight or so years old and in good health. Matt used a loop of lead rope to fashion a makeshift hackamore and leaped onto the bay's bare back to put it through its gaits.

"I'm satisfied," he said when he was done. "How d'you want to deal?"

"I'll take your horse in trade and seventy-five dollars cash. You can have your brother's horse and saddle. No charge for those."

"I expect you had to pay Espinosa a little gratuity of some sort when he gave you the bill of sale."

Tippett shrugged. "No matter."

"Even so, I want to reimburse you for that. And I'll take the bay. Tell you the truth, I would've paid more than that for him if you asked."

"Son," Tippett said with a groan, "don't never tell that to a horse trader. It takes all the pleasure out of the deal."

"Sorry, Mr. Tippett. I didn't mean to mess up your fun." Matt transferred his gear onto the bay horse, then saddled Sam's and tied a light lead to its bit.

"You could do one more thing for me if you would," Matt said as he swung into his saddle.

"You'll be wanting directions to Conquistador Mountain, I expect."

"Yes, sir, I guess I will."

"All right then. Here's what you do. . . ."

CHAPTER 19

"Stop!" The order was one Sam was perfectly willing—even eager—to obey. He came to a halt, as did Blue Runner on the other side of the arrastra bar.

The guard cradled his shotgun in the crook of his arm, lifted his hat, and used it to shade his eyes as he peered toward the sun. "Noon," he announced a moment later, having judged that by the sun's progress across the pale copper bowl of the sky.

Sam snorted softly under his breath. The guard was a foolish man. Rather than inflict upon himself the discomfort of looking into the sun, he could more easily and just as accurately determined the same thing by looking down instead. To the shadows that also gave testimony to the sun's progress.

"You!" The guard motioned to Blue Runner with the muzzle of his scattergun. "Unhook yourself and come over here. You." He pointed to Sam. "Take your ball off the bar and stand there."

Blue Runner staggered a little under the weight of the iron ball he was forced to carry, no doubt also because of the influences of fatigue and heat. The day was blaz-

ing hot and all three men, the guard included, were dripping wet with sweat.

When Blue Runner and Sam were standing side by
side, the guard nodded toward the flat plateau where the
buildings were. "March."

With Sam and Blue Runner leading the way and the
armed guard close behind, they moved up onto the bench
and across it to the building that seemed to be the headquarters. Despite the heat of the day there was smoke
coming from a stovepipe on the roof and the scent of
cooking food drifted into the yard.

The guard moved them past the building to a pair of
huge oaken barrels. Small buckets of the same sort that
food was served in were piled beside the barrels.

"Each of you fill a bucket," the guard ordered.

"Fill with what?" Blue Runner asked.

"There's water in the vats. Fill the buckets with that.
And take a dipper, each of you. There's dippers hanging
on some nails behind the vats. You'll see when you get
over there. You're gonna take water down to the men in
the pit. That's part of the job of the arrastra crew. You
gotta carry water to the other men. After all, you got the
easy job. They're the ones doing all the work."

Easy, Sam thought. Walking around in circles pushing a heavy crusher under a boiling hot sun for hour
after hour. Yeah. Easy. He picked up a bucket and a
dipper, and while he was engaged in filling the bucket
to carry down to the others, managed a drink for himself too. The water was as warm as spit but was
revitalizing in spite of that. He dumped another dip-
perful over his head, enjoying the feel of it trickling
down over his chest and across his ribs.

"Don't be wasting water or time neither," the guard
grumbled without sounding like he really meant it. But

then he was hot and likely bored as well. "Take those buckets down and let the others drink. Go on now. And don't forget, you're being watched every step of the way."

The shotgun guard remained on the lip over the open pit along with a pair of fellow guards while Sam and Blue Runner made their way down the narrow, winding path to the bottom of the pit where some sort of ore— Sam had no idea what the material was—was being extracted.

Making it to the bottom without falling was precarious business, Sam discovered, burdened as they were by the buckets in one hand and their iron balls and chains in the other. A slip near the top would likely be fatal. A fall from farther down the path would probably have resulted in a broken limb at the very least.

As they neared the bottom of the pit, Sam had the impression that they were descending into warm water rather than open air.

No hint of breeze could possibly reach the bottom, and the heat was stifling. It was difficult to breathe and he could feel the sun's burning heat like a heavy blanket laid over him on a torpid summer's day. It was no wonder that the men who were required to work down here glistened with sweat. And no wonder either why the guards made the effort to send water down. Having to work without water to replenish the fluids lost to sweat in heat like this would lead to sure heat stroke, even death.

Sam doubted very much that the men who ran this place cared a thing about the welfare of their workers.

But they surely cared very deeply that those laborers remain alive and capable of producing work.

Chunks of . . . something, he did not know what . . . were being extracted from the rock in this man-made pit on the mountainside. Obviously the stuff had to be valuable.

If, Sam thought, it could be mined cheaply enough. Probably the ore was of a low grade, not worth enough to justify paying a decent wage to professional miners. Or even to the peons who lived nearby.

But slave labor is as cheap as it is possible to get, and a corrupt system of so-called justice was capable of producing the necessary labor. That would explain why all the prisoners here—slaves was more like it—were Indians of one tribe or another.

The so called "wild tribes" had no legal standing on the Mexican side of the border, and the mine would likely accommodate as many as could be arrested down in San Iba, charged with almost anything, and then sentenced to hard labor, the mine owners likely paying the officer in charge of the local garrison for the services of his prisoners.

Sam had heard of such things before including in the southern part of his own United States.

But he had not expected to run into anything like it.

Somewhere up above a whistle blew and the men dropped their implements, picked up their balls and chains, and came limping as fast as they could to surround the water carriers and grab for the dipper handles.

Sam shuddered, thinking that soon he would be forced to work down here too. As bad as working the arrastra was, this was ten times worse. And the worst part of it all was the humiliation.

Sam August Webster Two-Wolves was and would always be a *warrior*. He would much prefer death to any other course.

Soon enough, he realized, he would have to make a choice between slavery and a warrior's proud death. Or more accurately, soon enough he would have to act upon the only true course that was open to him.

Unless Matt got here first.

CHAPTER 20

Matt felt a prickly tingle between his shoulder blades, and the hair on the back of his neck began to feel stiff. It was a sensation he had felt before. And on more than one occasion it was a feeling that saved his bacon.

On the other hand, sometimes when he'd felt this way, it was only a case of nerves. Sometimes nothing turned out to be wrong except his own worries.

Still, a man is a fool if he takes chances when an angel on his shoulder whispers warnings in his ear. He reined the bay horse off the wagon road and into some brush that was uphill from the right of way.

More curious now than concerned, Matt dismounted and tied both his horse and Sam's, then slipped down the slope to a position where he could remain concealed from anyone passing below but where he had a good command of the roadway.

If he needed it. That still remained to be seen. If anyone was following, they were doing a good job of keeping out of sight.

Matt very nearly decided that he was imagining things, that Sam's troubles simply had him spooked. He was about ready to turn and go back up to the horses when a faint sound reached his ears. The tick of a hoof on rock? He cocked his head over to one side and closed his eyes, listening intently and trying to filter out the faint sounds of life around him, the whir of a bee and the soft thrum of a dragonfly's wings, the leaf-rustle of a chipmunk or perhaps a mouse skittering through the grass, the soft soughing of a breeze flowing past pine needles.

There! He heard it again. More distinctly this time too.

Matt opened his eyes again in time to see the bob of a horse's head coming around a slight curve in the road in the direction from which he'd just come.

A gray horse came into view, the rider a dark, com-plected man wearing the broad hat and leather britches of a vaquero. The gray walked fully into view, and then a brown horse behind it, and soon after it a third.

The riders were all lean men with pistols on their hips and carbines carried balanced across their pommels.

Matt frowned when he saw that. He could clearly see that the horses carried rifle scabbards strapped onto their saddles. Yet those carbines were in the riders' hands, ready for quick action.

Somehow Matt did not think these men were out for an afternoon of hunting deer.

Somehow he did not think it a coincidence that they would be following silently behind him now.

Scowling, he hunkered low behind a screen of brush. Those riders held carbines ready while Matt's long gun was in its scabbard a good ten yards distant.

He waited, watching, while the vaqueros drew nearer.

The workers gulped down full dippers of the precious water, acting as if they were desperate for it, yet Sam could not help but notice that these men who represented very different tribes and immeasurably different cultures were meticulous in their concern that they take no more than was theirs and that the dipper quickly be passed to the next man in line.

"Good. Good," Nana kept saying between draughts of the refreshing fluid.

"You see what it is here," Koronado told Sam. "Tomorrow or the other tomorrow. You will work here. You will know then." He looked up toward the rim where the armed guards stood watching, and he spit out a word in his own tongue. Sam did not need to know the translation to understand the feeling that was behind it.

"Why do you work?" Sam asked. "Why do you do what they want of you?"

"I am not afraid," Koronado said, standing more fully upright and tossing his head defiantly. "I am Koronado and I am warrior."

"I understand that," Sam said, "but why do you do what they want? You said that no man lives to walk free from here. If that is so, then why do you stay, why do you work, why do you not kill a guard before one of them kills you or the work itself kills you?"

Koronado's expression hardened. But his eyes slid away from Sam's. The man felt shame, Sam suspected. Shame because he had not chosen a warrior's death over this servitude in chains.

"We have spoken of these things," Koronado mumbled after a moment. "Among ourselves. We talk. Of this. Of many things. In our bellies"—he thumped his chest with a fist—"in here each believes he will live to the end of the time the white man say must be served here. Each believes he will be the one who is strong, the one who . . . I do not have the Anglish word."

"The one who survives," Sam suggested.

"Yes. Survive. The one who survive. Each believe he will be that one. Will go home to wickiup. Hold his woman in the night and see his sons strong. Will again be free man. You know?"

"I know," Sam said.

And indeed he did. He too yearned for freedom. But if for one instant he truly believed that he would not live to achieve freedom again, he would prefer the warrior's proud death.

Sam paused a moment and braced himself while the men jostled for the dipper handle. Apparently their rules of peculiar etiquette ended once every man had received his first full dipper of water. After that it was every man for himself.

It occurred to him that this belief, this reaching for the luxury and the joy of freedom, was exactly what Koronado just explained. It was what kept the prisoners from bolting in a futile, self-destructive rush into the muzzles of the guns.

Each man in his heart believed he would somehow survive to be released and to return to his people, that he would again see his woman and his children.

It was not fear that held these men in check, Sam realized. It was hope.

And hope was a far more powerful thing than fear. In himself. In these men as well.

Sam tipped the bucket so the parched workers could get the last of the water, and when even that would not allow them to scoop anything into the dipper, he tilted the bucket and poured the last drops from it.

"That's enough lollygagging," one of the guards called down from the rim of the pit. "Git back to work. Do it now."

Reluctantly the prisoners shuffled back to their labors, the sweat that had glistened on their bodies already dried in the intense, furnacelike heat at the bottom of the ore pit. Soon enough they would be running wet with sweating again, though.

"You with the buckets. Get up here. This ain't no holiday for you neither."

Sam picked up the iron ball and cupped it in one hand while he carried the empty bucket in the other.

He began the steep, laborious climb back to the mountainside bench where the mine buildings lay.

And the guards. The guards with their shotguns and their scowls waited there too. Ah, if only. . . .

CHAPTER 21

Matt waited until the vaqueros were a few feet past, then stepped out into the road. "Are you boys looking for anyone in particular?"

He found it perversely amusing to note how sharply the three men jumped when they heard his voice behind them. One man very nearly dropped his carbine, and two of the horses tried to bolt when they felt the unexpected movement of their riders.

The men drew rein and stopped dead in the road. None of the three of them turned around to see who had spoken. If Matt needed any proof that these three were up to no good, he figured that right there was enough to give it. Innocent men—even if they thought they were being robbed—would surely turn around to see who was there. Whether he was alone. Whether there were guns pointed at them now. These three already knew. Or assumed they knew.

"You can drop your guns now. They aren't cocked. I can see that. They aren't going to go off from hitting the ground, so just open your hands and let them fall. The rifles first. We'll deal with your belly guns in a minute. Drop the carbines, boys. Do it *now!*"

Matt's voice hardened on the last word.

And as soon as the sounds were out of his mouth he moved sideways, back closer to the brush-covered hillside. He wanted to shift silently away from the point where he was last known to have been. Just in case.

Just in case the Mexicans did what in fact they did do.

The three sat where they were for a moment, their backs still toward Matt. But he could see from the movement of their heads and the working of their bearded jaws that they were talking softly among themselves.

If they were speaking Spanish they could as easily have laid their plans as loudly as they pleased and he would not understand a word. But then they would not know that. In fact, he did not know for sure that they spoke English and had understood his instructions. He hoped they had because he sure couldn't repeat the orders in Spanish for them.

They whispered for some moments, pretending not to; then at some signal that Matt did not see, the three of them moved, quickly and as one. All three yanked their horses around in a lightning spin.

At the same time all three whipped their carbine barrels forward, the short rifles held like pistols.

All three muzzles sought one target.

Except Matt was not standing where they expected him to be, where his voice had just come from.

One of the vaqueros was so keyed up, his hand was tightening on the trigger even before his carbine barrel came on line with the intended target. His rifle spit flame and death.

Spit futilely, the muzzle blast of hot gases from his carbine's discharge flashing beside the ear of the next rider's horse and spooking it into a head-down, hoof-flying explosion.

The bullet sailed somewhere down the road in the general direction of San Iba, miles distant.

That rider, or perhaps one of the others, cursed loudly in Spanish, while the man on the bucking horse grabbed for leather and dropped his carbine. The weapon was cocked and ready to fire and when the muzzle hit the ground, the jar dislodged the hammer sear and the gun went off, the force of that small, contained explosion driving the carbine upward to bang against the belly of the rider's already very unhappy horse.

The man lost complete control of his mount, and it went tearing down the road toward San Iba as if chasing after the first man's uselessly spent bullet.

Which left one armed man sitting astride a calm and steady horse and one very rattled man who carried a pistol in his sash and a rifle in his hands but whose carbine had a spent cartridge in the chamber, and whose hands were full from trying to manage both horse and rifle at the same time.

The one vaquero who was not rattled had a look of faint amusement on his lips. He shook his head very slightly and then smiled. "So, Señor Bodine. It is only you an' me now, is this not so?"

"You know who I am," Matt said.

"Aye, Señor. I have heard of you. I have heard you are a man who is with the fast gun. Is this not so?"

"Fast is a relative term," Matt told him.

"You still live, Señor Bodine."

"Yes, I reckon I do. Are you here working for Jarold Williams? Or for that lieutenant, whatever the heck his name is."

"Espinosa. The lieutenant's name is Espinosa."

"Thank you."

"Not that this information is of consequence. I do not work for any man, Señor Bodine." He grinned cockily. "Not at this moment, no. But I think maybe someone will pay me a small reward for having shot you, Señor. Someone is sure to thank me, and this will be to my advantage. And my honor."

"Ah, but you are forgetting one thing, Señor . . . what was your name again, sir?"

The vaquero laughed and took his hand off the grip of his carbine to thump his chest and proudly proclaim, "I am Juan Escobar Estero Garcia, Señor. Now, Señor, what is this thing that you say I forget?"

"Before you collect your reward, Juan, don't you reckon you should first do the job?"

"Oh. You mean I should shoot you before I make claim that your scalp belongs to me."

"Exactly."

Garcia spoke to the rider who was beside him, and that man looked unhappy with what he said but did not dispute it. He put the spurs to his horse and went galloping down the road in the direction where the third rider had disappeared.

"I have sent both my companions away, Señor. I want everyone to know that it was I who brought down the famous Señor Bodine and no other."

"I hate t' keep reminding you of the same old thing, Juan, but you haven't brought nobody down."

"Oh, but I will, Señor. I will." The man was grinning quite happily now. "Would you do me the honor to meet me *mano a mano,* Señor?"

"I don't know what that means," Matt said.

"In your language the expression would be face-to-face. It is not a translation, you understand. Our expression is hand-on-hand, but the meaning, it is the same."

"I see."

"Please allow me to put this clumsy rifle aside and to get down from my horse. I would not want your bullet to go astray and strike him when I shoot you, Señor. He is a good horse. Not so fast but very strong. Would you permit this?"

"Sure, Juan. Go right ahead if you like."

Garcia shifted his grip on the carbine so that he held it by the action, not the grip. He leaned down and slid the weapon into its scabbard and then, still smiling, stepped down from the horse. He shooed the animal off to the side, then dropped the reins to ground-tie it.

"So. *Gracias, Señor.* Thank you."

"You're quite welcome, Juan."

Garcia wore his pistol like a man who knew what to do with one. It was at a sensible height, neither dangling ridiculously low on his thigh nor perched up under his armpit, either extreme having its faults.

The Mexican tilted his head hard to one side and then to the other to loosen any tightness in his neck or shoulders. He drew in a long, deep breath and let it out again, smiling all the while.

"Do you wish a moment to pray, Señor?"

"No, thanks. But you go right ahead if you like."

Garcia closed his eyes. His lips moved and he mumbled softly under his breath for a few moments. When he opened his eyes again his expression was serious. And calm. He said, "I have prayed for your soul, Señor."

"And for your own, I hope."

"Yes, Señor. And for mine as well. Do you wish time to prepare?"

"I'm always prepared, Juan."

"In that case, Señor. . . ."

Garcia's hand flashed. He was quick. Fast as a striking rattler. He might even have been the fastest man Matt ever faced. Ever saw.

Matt was faster.

The first burning-hot slug from Matt's .45 ripped through Juan Garcia's throat half a heartbeat before the Mexican gunfighter's Colt cleared leather.

Garcia triggered his revolver, but it was due solely to the muscle contractions of a dead man. The gun fired into the ground at Garcia's feet.

There was one brief instant when something—shock, recognition of his own mortality, something—flickered in Garcia's bright eyes. And then the brightness, along with the life, went out of those eyes.

Garcia toppled face-forward onto the road. He made no effort to catch himself, and almost certainly was already dead before he hit the ground.

Matt gave a look back down the road, but there was no sign of the other vaqueros. He stood silently there for a moment, then flicked open the loading gate of his revolver.

He hoped Garcia's prayers had been heard.

With a sigh Matt picked up Garcia's revolver and stuffed it back into the man's plain and very businesslike holster. The kindest thing he could do now, he figured, would be to tie the body back on the horse and then turn the animal loose to return to wherever home was.

The whole thing seemed an awful waste.

But then dying generally did.

Waste or not, though, about all a man could do, Matt reflected, was to make sure he wasn't the one doing the dying.

CHAPTER 22

The bay horse began to stamp and fidget beneath him. Matt's hand curled back on the reins without conscious thought in reaction. He was pleased with the horse, but it would need to learn to stand steady for however long Matt chose. And right now he was much more interested in the view below him on the mountainside than he was in paying attention to a horse.

Matt had left the marked road a half mile or so behind and below, angling instead up a worn game trail that climbed a barren, rocky slope to this spot above Jarold Williams's old conquistador mine. From here he could get a look at the layout. At the open pit where men wearing balls and chains labored in killing heat. At a tunnel opening and collection of shacks that obviously had been built in recent years. And at a much smaller pit on a bench below the ledge where the mine was located.

It was this small pit that held Matt's interest now. In it two men were chained to either end of a timber that ran like an axle through a round stone wheel. The two were turning the wheel round and round inside this bowl-like depression, crushing ore that the other prisoners extracted from the mine.

One of those men was Sam August Webster Two-Wolves. In chains! His shirt ragged and torn, his back bloodied.

While Matt watched, the man on the other end of the axle pole called out something and tried to stop, but Sam continued pushing as if he hadn't heard.

More than likely, Matt realized, his brother indeed had not heard. Sam probably had retreated into himself, into a trancelike state of prayer and meditation where he spoke with his Cheyenne ancestors and invoked spirits Matt could only guess at. As close as Matt was to Sam and to the Cheyenne people, there were yet some places where he could not follow. Matt knew from past experience that when Sam was in one of those states, he was virtually impervious to outside influences, even pain.

There seemed to be only three men guarding the . . . how many? Nine prisoners total that Matt could see. And like Doc Tippett suggested, all the prisoners looked like Indians with dark skin and black hair. Their three guards all carried shotguns.

Matt was tempted to step down from the bay and find a nice spot where he could stretch out with his rifle and a firm rest from which to shoot. The three guards would go down like roosters being prepared for Sunday dinner, one, two, three. Matt could put the last one down almost before the first had time to hit the ground.

He was tempted, but he knew he would not do it. Not like that. For all he knew these men were hired in good faith and thought they were legitimately guarding desperadoes. Matt was not going to gun them down from ambush.

Although, seeing what had been done to Sam, it was almighty tempting.

Instead Matt dismounted and walked back to Sam's horse. He pulled the cinches tight, having left them a little loose for the horse's comfort and stamina while they traveled. Now, well, now he did not know if Sam might need to make a fast getaway, chains and all. If he did, he would not want to have to put up with a saddle slipping and flopping around under him.

Matt saw to Sam's cinches and tightened his own, then mounted again and headed back down the way he had come after he left the game trail. When he reached the road he turned up it in the direction of the mine.

A sign posted beside the road warned PRIVATE PROPERTY, NO TRESPASSING in English and Spanish—at least Matt assumed the Spanish words repeated the same warning—with a large skull-and-crossbones symbol to emphasize the message for those who could not read either language.

Matt paid the sign no mind.

Sam's chest swelled with a fierce joy that bubbled through his blood and roared in his ears as he saw his brother ride down from the trail. Matt had come. Of course.

"Hey, you! What'd you stop pushing for? I didn't tell you that you could take a rest."

Sam hadn't even realized that he had quit pushing the arrastra bar. He stood now watching Matt approach. Sam glanced at the guard with disdain, then motioned with his chin toward the lone horseman. The guard turned.

"The boss ain't here if it's work you're looking for," the guard announced when Matt was near.

"Thank you, but I've already found what I came for." Matt drew rein and stepped down from his horse. The guard looked puzzled, but not worried. After all, he had a shotgun. And he was in charge. He had no need for concern.

"Are you friends with one o' the fella? Virgil maybe? Are you the fella Virgil was drinking with the other night? Sorry, but visitors ain't welcome, mister. You'll have to go on back to town. But I can give Virgil a message for you if you want."

"I don't know anybody named Virgil, friend, and I'm not here to visit anyone. I'm here to get my brother."

"Your brother?" The guard looked confused.

Matt's smile was patient. "That's right. My brother."

"Who's your . . . mister, you don't mean one o' the prisoners, do you?"

"Yes, I do, friend. That one." Matt pointed.

"But you can't. . . ."

"Oh, I can. Trust me about this. I can and I will. Now where is the key to that ugly chain thing?"

"There's no key. It's welded. Not that it makes no difference. He ain't going anywhere. I'm here to see to it."

"Now, friend, I am trying to be nice about this," Matt said. His voice had a calm, almost lazy quality that Sam recognized. It meant that Matt was on a razor-thin edge.

Sam spoke up. "There is a blacksmith shack up by the mine. We should be able to find a hammer and cold chisel there." He grinned. "By the way, it's nice to see you, Matt. Now that you finally got here. Even though you took your own sweet time about it."

"See here, you two. I won't hear any more talk about cold chisels and stuff like that. This man is a prisoner of the *alcalde* of San Iba and it is my job to see that he stays right here," the guard protested.

"Sorry," Matt said. "He's coming with me."

"Over my dead body!" the guard responded, finally seeming to realize that he had a serious situation here.

"Friend, if that's the way you want it, then that is the way it can be," Matt told him. "But I want to warn you, if you thumb back the hammers on that scattergun of yours, I'll cut you down."

"You can't. . . ."

Matt's face went hard and his voice cold. "Trust me. I can."

"But. . . ."

"Lay the shotgun down and step very carefully away from it. You can go with us to the blacksmith shack. After you cut that chain off my brother you can go on your way. Alive. Or you can lie here dead and we will find the blacksmith shack without you. It's your choice."

The guard lifted the shotgun as if he was thinking about offering resistance. Matt's hand flashed and the guard found himself looking down the barrel of a Colt .45.

"My God, mister, don't shoot." The guard turned pale. Very quickly he bent and placed the shotgun on the ground at his feet.

"Thank you," Matt said. He holstered his revolver and motioned the guard away from the gun.

Sam lifted his chain down from the arrastra bar and held the heavy iron ball to his belly so he could walk up the hill with Matt. Sam's heart was soaring and he silently offered up some prayers of thanks to the spirits of his ancestors.

"Are you all right, Sam?"

"I will be. Now."

"You do pick the strangest ways to have fun," Matt said. "Must be the Indian in you."

"You white boys aren't the only ones who know how to have a good time, you know."

The unhappy guard walked nervously in front of Matt, and the Yaqui Indian Blue Runner was coming up the hill behind them. Blue Runner was struggling to carry his iron ball and the guard's shotgun, which he had picked up and brought along.

"Over there," the guard said, indicating the blacksmith shack.

"Lead the way," Matt ordered. "You can take those chains off."

"Off him too," Sam put in, aiming his thumb at Blue Runner. "He's a friend."

"Him too," Matt agreed.

"Now looka here. . . ." The guard's protest sputtered out and faded away. He opened the doors to the blacksmith shop and picked up a hammer and chisel.

With the proper tools it took little to break the welds and remove the ankle strap from Sam and then from Blue Runner.

"You fellas are going to be in an awful lot of trouble once Mr. Williams and the *alcalde* hear about this," the guard said. He placed the chisel and hammer back onto the bench where he'd found them. "You know I'll have to tell them who done this."

"Tell them whatever you please," Matt said. He smiled at the man and slapped him on the back. "Just remember that you're alive to be able to tell them."

"Yes, sir."

Matt turned to Sam. "What about those other men down inside that hole out there?"

"I think Blue Runner is already doing something about that," Sam said. The Yaqui had taken the shotgun and trotted away in the direction of the pit as soon as he was free from the ball and chain.

Sam heard a distant shout and then a sequence of dull, booming explosions. Shotguns. More than one. Four shots, then a fifth. And then silence.

Sam ran to the rim of the pit and saw carnage below. Blue Runner was dead, cut down by a charge of buckshot, but so was one of the two guards. The other guard was either dead or dying. The prisoners were standing over the man, battering him with the terribly heavy iron balls attached to their leg chains. By the time Sam and the others got to the pit, there probably was not an unbroken bone remaining in the guard's body and it seemed very unlikely that he could still be alive.

The Indians, Sam knew, would soon enough come up and free themselves from their chains. They would disappear into the mountains like smoke on a freshening breeze.

Sam turned to the one remaining guard. "If you know what's good for you," he said, "you'd best hightail it out of here or else find a good place to hide."

"Oh, God! Oh, Jesus. I think I'm gonna be sick." The guard spun away from the sight of his dead friends. He was trembling so hard it seemed difficult for him to stand. But he managed to break into a shuffling trot and then into a hard run.

Sam turned to Matt. He grabbed Matt's forearm so that once again, as it had been so very long ago, their wrists touched together at the place where their blood had flowed into one stream. "It is good that you came," he said.

"Yes," Matt said with a warm, brotherly smile. "Yes, I reckon it is at that."

The two turned toward their horses.

CHAPTER 23

The two sat hunkered beside a tiny campfire that was no larger than the pot that sat over it. The rich aroma of boiling coffee surrounded them, as did the sound of trickling water. Sam had found a spot where spring-water seeped out of the rock and flowed in a miniature waterfall into a small pool. The beauty of the tiny glen had nothing to do with why they'd stopped, however. The brothers had much to catch up on.

"The man's name is Case Wilhelm."

"Case? Where would that come from?" Matt asked.

Sam shrugged, his powerful shoulders glistening with cold water from the pool. One of the first things he'd done when they got here, even before Matt had the fire together, was to strip and bathe the sweat and grime of captivity from his body. It might take more than a simple bath to remove the memories from his mind. He said, "Short for Casey would be my guess, but I could be wrong."

Matt smiled. "You? Wrong? Impossible."

"Yeah, you would think so, wouldn't you," Sam said. "Anyway, whatever the man's name, we will see each other again. Count on it. Except this time I won't be in chains."

He paused. "And it will make no difference at all if there are men standing by with shotguns to protect him."

"The bunch that was down there today sure won't be with him. Those Indians. . . ." Matt grimaced. "What they did to the guards was sheer savagery."

"And what the guards had done to them was sheer evil," Sam reminded his brother. "Down here Indians are regarded as vermin, Matt. There is no longer a bounty for our scalps and ears, but it is considered no crime to kill an Indian. I cannot find it in my heart to condemn those men." He smiled. "Even if they were Yaqui and Apache while everyone knows that the only true human beings are us Cheyenne."

"It's just lucky that I became a Cheyenne then, isn't it?" Matt said, his voice light.

Sam's expression, however, became serious. "Yes, my brother. It is truly fortunate." Sam sighed. "Hand me that shirt, will you?"

"That's your good shirt. You aren't gonna wear that for everyday, are you?"

"That is my best shirt. It is also my only shirt. Last one left. I need to buy some more."

"Fine, but I don't recommend you doing any shopping in San Iba."

Sam poured coffee for both of them and handed one cup to Matt. He settled the pot close beside the little smokeless fire but not directly over it, wanting to keep the coffee hot but not boiling. "You know, brother, there are times when I become disgusted with our government in the United States. Bureaucrats can be stupid at times and corrupt. It makes me furious. But every now and then something will happen to make me remember and to appreciate the freedoms that we Americans take for granted."

"Like now," Matt said.

"Yes. Exactly like now. In America even an Indian or a black man is regarded as a human being with the right to life and whatever happiness he can find for himself. Even an Indian can be respected. And even a scrawny white boy can learn to make an acceptable cup of coffee."

"Acceptable? Acceptable, is it? This coffee is magnificent." Matt reached to grab Sam in a wrestling hold, then pulled back when he saw the raw, ugly welts on his brother's back. "Ouch. Does that hurt?"

"I am Cheyenne. I am impervious to pain."

"Yeah I know that, but does it hurt?"

"Like the very devil," Sam said, wincing.

"I have a little salve in my saddlebags. I'll grease you up before you put your good shirt on. If you're gonna wear the thing for everyday, you might as well get it grubby right off the bat. Why wait?"

"I know I can always come to you for advice, my brother. And I know to always do the opposite of what you suggest. Now you have heard my sad tale of woe. Tell me what you have accomplished. Why wasn't Pete with you, for instance? What is the reason he asked us to come here to begin with?"

Matt filled Sam in on his recent activities and added that, "No one seems to know what has happened to Pete. Nothing that they'll admit to anyway."

Sam shook his head. "I think I may know where Peter is now."

"Fine. Let's go get him. Anita and Ricardo are eaten up with worry about him going missing like this."

"Unfortunately, Matt, I'm thinking Peter may be 'down the hill.'"

"Like I said, let's go get him."

"You misunderstand, brother. To the ones who are

forced to slave in that mine, 'down the hill' has a harsh meaning." Sam explained the crude disposal method for the Indians who died under the lash there.

"Why would you think Pete might be down this hill then?" Matt asked.

"At night while we ate and for a little while afterward we talked. Sometimes they included me in the conversations or at least spoke in English so I could understand. The Apaches mentioned that there were some Mexicans who were sent down the hill. And there was a white man. Not many days before Blue Runner and I were captured, the big owner of the mine. . . ."

"That would be Jarold Williams. He's the man in town who was so helpful to me with that Mexican Army officer. I told you about him. He's a snake in the grass, but he helped me out that time."

"Yes, and I believe he 'helped' me as well. I think he may be the man who sent for this Lieutenant Espinosa to arrest me. At any rate, he is the big boss. The Apache said one day this big boss and Espinosa and two soldiers came. They had a white man with them but this white man was handcuffed.

"Nana's friend Tomas was pushing the arrastra that day, he and one of the Yaquis. The men on the arrastra were taken off the push bar and sent up to the mine with the Mexican soldiers so none of them could see. They heard nothing for a long while; then there were two gunshots. After that the big boss and Lieutenant Espinosa came up to the mine and the Indios were sent back down to finish the job of crushing ore in the arrastra.

"There was no sign of the white man, but Tomas said some of the piled ore they were supposed to crush was gone. Down the hill. It had to be because no one carried it away. The white man was killed and sent down the hill, then his body was covered with tailings and even with some of the good ore. Tomas was pleased because it meant he had less work to do that day to make their quota at the arrastra."

"He cared nothing for the dead white man?"

"Tomas is Apache. Tomas cares for Apache. But he was good to me even though I am Cheyenne. He helped take care of me when I was hurt."

"Then I'm grateful to him," Matt said. "You really think that could've been Pete they murdered?"

"They were not specific about the days, but from what you tell me about Pete's disappearance, I believe the timing fits."

"This is gonna be hard on Anita. You haven't met her yet, but you'll like her. She's a fine girl. Deep in love with Pete, though. Losing him, it'll be tough."

"Life is tough," Sam said, "and it is not fair. She has the boy and there is a child on the way. She has family. She will turn to them, and they will all do the best they can. As for us. . . ."

"Yeah," Matt said. "We're gonna do the best we can too. For Pete an' for you too, Sam. I reckon we are gonna have to find a way to make it clear to those fellas that murdering folks an' making slaves of them ain't a nice thing to do."

"Do you think we should smite them, Matt?"

"With gusto," Matt said, grinning. He finished his coffee and poured another cup, then with an innocent expression asked, "When that time comes, Sam, can I borrow your jawbone please?"

"My. . . ." It took a moment for Matt's request to sink in. Then Sam broke into loud, guffawing laughter.

CHAPTER 24

"I have been thinking."

"That always worries me 'cause it usually means trouble, but I know you're gonna bust if you don't spit out whatever it is you're chewing on. Go ahead. Tell me."

"I have been thinking about Pete."

"Yeah. This is gonna be hard on Anita."

"We do not really know that it was Pete that they killed and buried here."

"No, I reckon we don't." Matt reached for the coffee-pot again, enjoying the aroma in the crisp, predawn air as much as the flavor of the dark brew.

"I should have thought of this last night," Sam said. "Now it is too late."

"For what?"

"I think we should find Pete. We should take him home to his family so they can make their prayers over him and see his spirit safely on its way. Besides, we do not truly know that it was Pete who was murdered there that day. Consider how terrible it would be for us to tell his wife that he is dead only to have him turn up next week or next month or next year."

"I would think she'd be happy to be wrong about that news."

"Yes, but then she would know the pain of his death twice, once now and again when someday it really happened. No, I think we must find that body and if it is Pete, we should take him home to his family."

Matt peered into the pale glow that rimmed the eastern horizon and took a moment to think about what Sam was saying. He took a swallow of his coffee, then nodded. "Makes sense. Much as I hate to admit it. But that slope is bare, and by now that overseer and the rest of the guards oughta be back at the mine. There's no prisoners for them to put to work, but they'll be mad. They'll be on the prod today, Sam, and there is no place t' hide on that bare rocky slope."

"Today will not be wasted," Sam said. "Tonight you will keep watch while I go down and look for Pete."

"Now wait just a minute. You can't. . . ."

"Whoa!" Sam said, holding his palm up to cut short the flow of objections that Matt was sure to make. "I know what you intend to say, but listen to the truth before you speak. As much as I hate to admit this, Matt, between the two of us you are the better shot, quicker with the pistol by half a heartbeat and straighter with the rifle by half a hair. That is true."

"Nice o' you to admit it."

"Now you should admit something else that is true. I have the gift of stealth and silence in a way that you never will. Oh, you are good, Matt. For a white man you are the best I have ever seen. But I am better."

"All right, brother, playfulness aside, I reckon that's the bald truth. Mist drifting over top o' the grass makes more noise than you do."

"Good. We are in agreement about this."

Matt nodded.

"Today I think you should ride to town. Buy supplies. We have nothing to eat here but a few scraps of jerky gathering lint in the bottoms of our saddlebags, and this is the last of the coffee too. Looking for Pete may take some time. I will have to dig through unstable rock to look for him and must do it without making sounds. We do not know how long we will be so we should prepare." Sam smiled. "Besides, I need new clothes."

"Sam, if you think you are gonna ride into San Iba and . . ."

"No, foolish brother. That would not be wise. I will wait here. I will wait where I can watch the mine. It will be good to know how many are there. And who they are."

"You're thinkin' about that overseer, aren't you?"

"Yes," Sam said, his expression suddenly hard. "I am."

"Do you want to take him now? We can go down right now and see if he's there, see if he has nerve enough to face you when you aren't in chains."

"No, Matt. Thank you. I know you would be there to back me up if this is what I chose to do. But no. We will see to Pete and his widow first. This thing with Case Wilhelm is personal. It can wait." Sam smiled but there was no hint of mirth in the expression now. His smile was cold. And as hard as gunmetal. "It will give me time to look forward to the pleasure of facing him man-to-man."

Matt looked at this dark, powerful man who was his brother, and a chill rushed through him. If he did not know Sam and trust him with his life, it would be easy to fear him when he was like this, distant and cold and turning inward to places where even Matt could not follow.

They sat like that in silence until the sun lifted free of the horizon and their campfire was reduced to ash. Finally, though, Sam Two-Wolves returned from whatever distant land he had been visiting. It happened in the blink of an eye. One moment Sam squatted in stony silence beside the dead fire. The next moment his dark eyes were full of life and warmth. His face split into a wide smile and he reached out to touch Matt on the shoulder in a brotherly gesture. "Come. We are wasting time here. Go to town, Matt. Get what we need. I will find a place where I can keep watch over the mine. I want to know how many are there and what their movements are now that they have no more slaves."

Matt nodded and reached for the coffeepot to pack it away.

CHAPTER 25

San Iba was a good four-hour ride from the small sweetwater pool where the brothers agreed to meet later in the day. Matt judged it was nearing eleven A.M. when he reached the town. He rode on through to the livery, where he turned his horse over to Doc Tippett.

"Give him some grain if you would please, Doc," Matt said, "and if you have time you might prepare a couple small sacks of grain that I can carry with me. I'd also like to rent that little mule you have and a pack-saddle to put on him. I'll pay whatever your rate is."

Tippett eyed Matt in silence for a moment, then sighed and said, "The people in town here have been told to be wary of you, son. They say there was some sort of ruckus out at Jarold Williams's mine yesterday. No one I've talked to knows the details, but everyone says you are suspected."

"I did nothing wrong, Doc. Did nothing to harm any man, not even in self-defense. I can tell you what happened, though. There was a revolt by the prisoners out there. They killed some of the guards and escaped into the mountains. I doubt anyone will ever see them again, not around here anyway."

"Is that so." The old man scratched inside his whiskers, then inspected his fingernail when he was satisfied that the itch had been quelled.

"Yes, sir, it's the truth. You might hear some fanciful accounts, but what I've just told you is what actually happened."

"You sound sure about it," Tippett said.

"I am. I was close by when it happened."

"Close by," Tippett repeated with a twinkle in his eye.

"Yes, sir."

"Then you should know." Tippett picked up the reins of Matt's bay. "I'll grain this horse, then get the mule ready to travel. They will both be ready by the time you get done with whatever it is you need to do."

Matt's first order of business was to find a good meal. He was on the verge of starvation. Or felt like it anyway. Everything considered, however, he did not much feel like taking his meal at the hotel where Jarold Williams and his friends were often seen, or at the nearby saloon. Instead he walked the short length of San Iba and pushed through the hanging fly beads that covered the door of a small, low-roofed cantina.

He knew immediately that he had come to the right place. In addition to a roly-poly little Mexican behind the bar, there was a remarkably pretty girl engaged in animated conversation with three vaqueros at a table in the back. Matt chose a seat where he had a good view across the room. Yessir, that was a very pretty girl.

The bartender said something and the girl patted one of the vaqueros on the wrist, gave the young man a pretty smile, and left the table. She was still smiling when she approached Matt.

"Sí, señor?"

"I'd like something to eat, please. Whatever you have; I'm not fussy. And a beer to wash it down."

"Frijoles, señor?"

Matt raised an eyebrow. "Free, uh . . . what was that you said?"

She laughed. "Beans, Señor. Will beans be good?"

"Beans. Sure. D'you have some meat to go with that? Beef, maybe?" He had no idea what the word for beef would be in Spanish.

"Meat, yes. No beef today."

Matt shrugged. "I'll take it, but I think maybe I'll be happier if you don't tell me what it is."

"You will like it. This I promise."

She was right too. Whatever the meat was—he suspected goat or possibly young lamb—it was good, tender and tasty. It went well with the beans. Those were so hot with spices that it was a wonder they didn't burst into flame, but they were good, and the beer cut some of the heat off Matt's tongue. He enjoyed his meal. Enjoyed the view at the other end of the room too where the girl returned to sit with the vaqueros.

Matt was just finishing his meal when the fly beads clacked merrily and the room darkened slightly from the intrusion of a man's figure into the doorway. Matt recognized him. This was one of the men who had been with Jarold Williams the day that tough-talking, slow-drawing gunfighter braced Matt in Tim's saloon.

For a moment Matt thought he might be in for another fight, but the fellow's intentions turned out to be harmless. He walked to the bar and briefly spoke with the short, chubby Mexican there. Then the proprietor fumbled beneath the bar for a moment. He produced a dark, slender cigarillo and handed it to the American, who paid for the cheroot and left without another glance in Matt's direction.

There was something about the man, though, something about the way he carried himself, a certain stiffness in the set of his shoulders and in the way he walked . . . it sharpened Matt's senses and left him on edge.

Matt quickly stood and dropped a coin on the table to pay for his meal.

Of a sudden he wanted to get his shopping done and hightail it out of San Iba before there was more trouble here. He already had enough of that on his plate for the moment, thank you.

On the other hand, it is not always a man's own choice.

CHAPTER 26

Sam Two-Wolves watched with amusement as a coney, one of the little short-eared rabbits that live in the rocks of the high country, made a meal from a sprig of grass. The fat little thing looked like it hadn't a care in the world. But of course it did. It had to be constantly vigilant against hawks and owls, bobcats and coyotes, snakes and who knows what else down here in this distant and foreign land. And constant vigilance can be a difficult thing to maintain.

That was a lesson Sam reminded himself of often. He had to. He had been lying here atop a slab of dark basalt for most of the morning, watching an empty mine site about two hundred feet below.

Case Wilhelm and half a dozen of his men were there—Sam had seen them earlier—but they were inside one of the several flimsy buildings left behind when the mine was last abandoned. Sam easily recognized several of the guards from his own confinement. They made him itch to pick up his rifle.

This was not about him, though. He and Matt were here to help Pete and his wife. Or his widow. Sam's face, already impassive, turned to granite at that thought. Whether the woman was a widow or not was something that needed to be determined. Then Sam and Matt could work out what needed to be done from there.

If the truth be known, however, Sam's hope was that they would find a time and a way when he could face Case Wilhelm face-to-face and man-to-man, just the two of them, with no chains to prevent Sam from taking Wilhelm's throat in his hands and . . .

Sam's attention suddenly took sharp focus. Something . . . he squeezed his eyes shut for a brief moment to clear them, then brought his attention to a jumble of sharp rocks below his position on the mountainside.

Something had moved there. He was sure of it. Well, almost sure.

Something other than the coney—it was gone now, vanished into its burrow with a flick of its tailless rump—something other than the family of young pygmy rattlesnakes that lived in the hollow thirty feet or so farther down the mountainside.

That hollow would have been a better position to watch from, hidden from the sides as well as from down on the shelf where the ancient mine was, but the presence of those deadly little snakes kept Sam up here out of harm's way.

He did not see the deadly little rattlers now, but . . .

Oh, my!

There was a patch of color where before there had been none.

Once he realized that, Sam was able to make the leap of recognition so sudden and clear, that it was startling to realize he hadn't seen it before. It was as if a still-life painting had been hanging before him but covered with a veil, and now the veil fell away.

Color, texture, form. All were there. Combined they added up to a recognizable figure that, once seen, made him amazed that he hadn't seen it earlier.

A human form. Clothed in drab colors. Dark flesh and black hair. Wearing a dark cap that Sam almost but not quite recognized. And then did. It was a U.S. infantryman's kepi with the shiny black visor cut or torn off and the brass medallions removed.

Sam could not get a good look at the owner of the cap except to see that he was small, perhaps a half-grown child. An Apache more than likely, judging by the clothes he wore. And by the hours upon hours of stoic immobility that had kept him unnoticed even by Sam's wary eyes.

Like a puzzle in the Sunday rotogravure, once it was seen, it was difficult to remember why and how the picture had not been obvious to begin with. After all, he was lying there in plain sight.

It occurred to Sam that if anyone were watching from farther up the mountainside, he himself would likely be just as invisible until or unless he moved.

Obviously this observer was watching the same scene that Sam was.

But for what reason? That was a question.

A mine guard down below provided the answer.

A door creaked open. Despite the distance, the sound of squeaking hinges easily reached Sam and alerted him before the first hint of movement down on the ledge where the mine was sited. One of the guards, not one Sam recognized, came into view when he stepped around to the side of the building where Wilhelm and the others were. The man unbuttoned his fly and proceeded to relieve himself against the sun-dried wood of the old mine shack.

Sam's attention was drawn much closer when the person lying in the rocks just below him quickly moved, reaching into a spot Sam could not see from his hiding place and lifting out a rifle.

The weapon looked almost but not quite familiar, and it took Sam a moment to recognize it. It was a musket, a muzzle-loading rifle of the sort that had been used in the War Between the States back in the white men's country. It looked very much like the current Army-issue Springfield .45-70, except these antiques lacked the flip-up trapdoor that enabled the shooter to load cartridges. This old rifle looked like it had seen both use and abuse in the years since it was new.

That did not prevent the person below from resting the barrel on a slab of rock and taking careful aim on the mine guard down below.

Sam did not particularly want a gunshot to bring the guards swarming out and starting a search of the mountainside up here.

But if it happened, it happened.

And if it happened, he just might be forced to shoot Case Wilhelm.

From a distance like this was not the way Sam hoped to face the man, but of course he would if need be. That was up to a power much greater than he.

Sam lay where he was, watching and waiting.

Wondering too. Wondering why there was no burst of smoke and boom of large-caliber gunshot.

The guard buttoned his trousers and ambled back around to the front of the building and out of the line of sight from the mountainside.

Sam's attention shifted to the small figure with the rifle.

He understood when he saw the figure move.

The would-be shooter rolled over, clutching his wrist.

A short, ugly pygmy rattler clung there, its fangs buried in flesh.

The rattler fell away and disappeared into a crack in the rock.

And Sam got his second surprise.

The would-be shooter was a girl. A young woman probably out of her teens. A rather pretty young woman at that.

Sam could see that she was angry now. He could not be sure, but she seemed less concerned with the potentially deadly snakebite than she was with the fact that her intended victim had gotten away.

She lifted the ancient rifle and sighted down the barrel. For a moment Sam thought she was going to shoot blindly into the roof or back wall of the mine shack in the blind hope of striking someone or something inside. Instead she only grimaced and carefully let the hammer of the old gun down to half-cock.

Then she peered closely at her wrist. Her flesh took on something of a clammy pallor under the dark copper of her skin, and she glanced with obvious regret at the tableau below her on the mountainside.

After a moment she picked up her antique Springfield and began very slowly and carefully making her way uphill.

If she continued on this path, her course would take her right over top of Sam August Webster Two-Wolves.

CHAPTER 27

Matt knew he was in trouble the moment he walked into the general store. All conversation stopped. All movement came to a halt. The customers in the place, mostly women but a few men as well, stood as still and as silent as statues, stood peering across the dark and musty room toward this intruder from across the border.

And it was not that they were unaccustomed to seeing Americans. More than half of these customers were Americans themselves. Besides, no one had acted that way a few days earlier when Matt came in asking if anyone knew where his brother was.

Everyone then had been smiling and pleasant. Now they looked like they expected a gunfight to break out at any moment.

And very likely they did.

The proprietor gave Matt a stricken look, as if he wished he'd had sense enough to hang a CLOSED sign in the window two minutes earlier.

It was too late for that now, though. Matt gave a nod and a polite tip of his hat to a clutch of Mexican women standing by the yard goods, and another to a pair of white ladies whose gossip had been interrupted by Matt's arrival.

"Good, uh, goo . . . um . . ." The storekeeper cleared his throat and tried again. "Good morning, sir."

Matt smiled and gave a cheery "Good morning" in return.

"What can I . . . uh, what, uh. . . ."

"I'll be needing some supplies. For travel, like. You know, the usual thing. Dry staples, maybe a few cans of sweet fruits for special. Cherries or peaches or like that. Jerked meat, not fresh. Some coffee already roasted and ground. Oh, and don't forget a few cans of milk and some sugar if you please."

"Yes, sir. Right away, sir."

"Oh, you needn't rush on my account," Matt said with a twinkle in his eye. "All these folks were here ahead of me. I don't mind waiting my turn."

"No, I, um, they are just visiting." He licked his lips and gave a tug to his shirt collar. "I have time to wait on you now."

"Whatever you think," Matt said with another smile.

"I'll only be a minute."

"Take your time." Matt ambled across the room to admire some ready-made shirts that were piled on a shelf. He checked the sizes by holding them up against his own torso, then with a half-hidden grin chose the three most garish and gaudy among them for Sam. One, a truly awful concoction of green and orange and blue, was so magnificently hideous that he had to have it for his blood brother. He had to wonder, though, just how shirts like these had come to be here. And how long they had been on the shelf.

Surely the drummer who sold them to the owner of this store must be a legend among traveling salesmen.

Matt got those, and some jeans that would fit Sam and some socks as well, the socks being for himself, and a couple extra pairs in case Sam needed some too.

By the time Matt was done picking out the clothing he wanted, the shopkeeper had his food order put together and waiting on the counter, already packed in sturdy jute bags suitable for travel. Wishful thinking perhaps.

Matt looked at the bags and realized that between the food and the clothing there would be more than one armload. And Doc Tippett's livery was down at the edge of town.

"I'll be back in a few minutes with a mule to load this onto. But I can pay you for it now if you like."

"Oh, uh, whatever you wish. Anything at all. Just . . . just take it on credit if you want."

Matt gave the man a questioning glance. This storekeeper did not know Matt from Adam's off ox. Obviously he was more interested in getting Matt out of his store—and himself out of the line of fire if there should be any—than in being paid for his wares.

"Now will be fine." Matt pulled some coins out of his pocket. "How much, please?" He had to ask the question twice before he got an answer.

He encountered no trouble—and practically no human beings—on his way down to the livery.

Siesta, Matt told himself. The streets of San Iba were empty because it was siesta time.

Except it was still early for siesta, and the American residents of the town were unlikely to observe that delightful Mexican habit to begin with.

"Quiet," Matt muttered as he snapped tight the cinches on the bay and took up the lead rope of the little mule.

"Whatever will happen," Tippett said, "it won't be in

town. I saw Lieutenant Espinosa and his soldier boys riding out toward the east."

"And Jarold Williams's gunfighters?" Matt asked. "What about them?"

"Funny you should ask. I noticed them heading west a little while ago."

West was the direction Matt needed to go in order to return to the mine and to Sam. He grinned. "Thanks, Doc. I owe you."

"Yes, you do," Tippett said with a nod. "Twenty-five cents for graining your horse and a dollar rental for the mule."

Matt felt good as he led horse and mule up the street to fetch his supplies and build the pack. He felt loose. Not eager exactly, but certainly ready if—when—Jarold Williams's gunmen chose to turn the wolf loose.

CHAPTER 28

The girl's attention was focused on the mine buildings below. And on the wrist where the snake bit her. She was pale beneath the copper of her skin and obviously very frightened. She slipped around the slab of stone where Sam was hiding and dropped to the ground behind it without ever turning her head—and a rather pretty head it was, Sam observed—to see where she was going.

She crouched there out of sight from anyone below but within four or five inches of touching Sam.

The girl held the musket in her left hand. It was the right where the snake had struck her.

Sam wanted to help her. Intended to help. The problem was managing to do so without startling her into a scream or gunshot or some other signal that might be heard down at the mine. The mountainside where they now were afforded countless opportunities for hidden observation . . . but almighty few escape routes should a group of armed and angry men become aware that there were people up here spying on them.

Sam felt he had little choice about how to announce

his presence. He reached over and clapped one hand over her mouth and pulled, rolling her against his chest so that his arms were wrapped tight around her slim form.

The result was an explosion of fury. But a contained explosion. Her cries—curses probably—were muffled.

Enough sound got out to let Sam know in no uncertain terms just how angry she was, but not so much that it would be heard down at the mine. At least he hoped not.

He also hoped her struggles were not for the purpose of securing a knife so she could stab him and get away. He had not seen any weapon other than the old musket. That did not mean she had none, only that he had not specifically seen any.

Sam held her arms tight to her sides, and eventually she seemed to realize that she had neither the strength nor the leverage to overcome his hold. She quit squirming and went to the other extreme, going limp in his grasp.

Much better, Sam thought. Now to try to explain. But in what language. He did not even know what tribe this girl belonged to. Her mode of dress suggested she might be Apache, but for all Sam knew she could as easily be Yaqui or Pima, or for that matter could belong to some tribe he'd never heard of. Mexico's native population was a complete mystery to a boy from the beautiful northern grasslands.

Sign language? Perhaps. But that involved the use of the hands, and he did not think it would be a good idea to turn her loose when she was in a fighting mood.

He had his own compellingly lovely Cheyenne tongue, of course. And a little Lakota. Some Arapahoe and Crow and a little Piegan. But he did not have a word of Spanish nor of a language of any of the southern tribes.

The girl seemed to be having trouble breathing, so Sam slightly relaxed the hand that covered her mouth. He shook his head. "I sure wish I knew how to talk to you," he mused aloud.

The girl stiffened again. Then twisted her head a little so she could peer up at him out of the corner of her eye. She lay trapped within his grasp for a little while, then again relaxed.

"You speak English," she whispered past the obstruction of his palm.

Sam recoiled as if he were the one who was snakebit. "Yes, of course."

"Let go of me," she said, her voice calm now. "Do not be afraid. I will not hurt you."

The idea of a slip of a girl like this hurting him was so ludicrous that Sam began to laugh. "You would harm me, you say?"

"If I had to, yes."

"How?"

"I would find a way. Just as I will find a way to make those white men suffer."

"Why would you do that, little sister?" Sam relaxed his grip on the girl and backed away from her. But he kept a very close eye on her hands lest she grab up the old rifle or pull a knife from somewhere on her person.

Not, actually, that there was very much of her person that he had not already been in close contact with when he'd had his arms wrapped so tight around her.

"They took my husband for a slave. He did nothing to harm them. He went to their town. He tried to buy medicine for our baby. They took him and made of him a slave."

"You have a baby?" Sam asked. The girl seemed much too young to have a child. But then perhaps the customs of her tribe were very different from what Sam was used to.

"I have a child no longer." Her voice was calm and flat. "The baby of my husband is dead. She did not have the medicine that he tried to buy in their town. She died. I must tell my husband and I must make the man pay who caused her death."

"I am sorry to hear of your loss, little sister. May I ask the name of your husband?"

"You would not know him. You are not of our people."

"And your people would be?"

"The white men call us Apache."

"I am of the Cheyenne," Sam said. "We have heard of the bravery of the Apache." They had heard other things about the Apache too, but he did not think this would be the best time or place to go into that. Besides, the Apaches with whom he was imprisoned had helped him when he was in need. He was in their debt.

"Your husband," Sam said. "May I know his name?"

"He is called by the name Koronado. He is a warrior and a good husband. Now he wears the chains of the white men, but someday . . . someday he will come home to me."

Sam grunted. "I know your husband. He is indeed a good man. Do you not know that he is free now? He and the others escaped from this place."

"This is true?" the girl asked.

"Indeed. Your husband was good to me when I was sick and wore the chains of those white men. I owe him a great debt. May I make a very small payment against that debt by helping his wife now that she is in need?"

"How do you mean?"

"Let me take you back to our camp. The camp of my brother and myself. The poison of that snake has been in you too long already. I will take out as much of it as I can, but you are sure to be sick for a time and very weak. Let us take care of you while you are in need."

Sam slid his knife out of its sheath and offered it to the girl. "You can make the cuts yourself if you do not trust me to do it."

She looked at the sharp blade and then into Sam's eyes. Then she took a deep breath and squeezed her eyes tight shut. "Help me," she whispered, her voice now that of a young and very frightened girl. "Help me, please."

CHAPTER 29

Matt's attention was focused on his horse much more than on his surroundings, but it was the mule that tipped him off. The little fellow's long, furry ears waggled and pointed toward the hillside above the wagon road and then flopped back flat against its head. Whatever the mule saw up there it definitely did not like.

Of course it might just be a catamount lurking up there. But Matt doubted that. More likely the predator— or predators; he did not know how many to expect—was of the two-legged kind.

He rode straight on for a moment more while he quickly assessed the surroundings. The road here passed through a scattering of young quaking aspen, then below a rocky overhang. Matt was betting that the ambush was set up on top of that overhang. Probably they intended to take him from behind when he passed beyond it. From the top of that rock formation anyone passing below would be a fish in a barrel. They couldn't miss.

Well, unless he didn't ride blindly beneath them.

And if Matt and the mule were wrong about this, no harm would be done other than the loss of a little time.

Better to prepare for a dozen attacks that failed to materialize than to ignore one warning of the real thing.

He waited until he was at least partially screened from that direction by a clump of pale aspen, then angled sharply off the wagon road and slipped silently to the ground. Tying his horse and the mule to a tree, Matt slid his Winchester out of its scabbard and checked to make sure there was a cartridge in the chamber, then rolled the hammer back to safe-cock. He also took a moment to scratch the hollow beneath the mule's jaw and give it a pat on the neck by way of a thank-you.

"Wait here, boys," he murmured before he hefted the carbine and started up the slope. He wanted to pick a route well up the hillside so he could come down on top of that rocky outcrop ahead, giving him the advantage if someone just happened to be there. Up there taking the sunshine perhaps. Or praying. Yeah. Right.

Three, four . . . no, five. Matt was flattered that they felt he deserved such a large honor guard. But then the fellow who was in charge had seen him shoot before. This was the other of the pair of run-down American gunmen who had been with the man named Curly when he braced Matt in the saloon a few days earlier. Someone had spoken to this one. Called him Lawrence if Matt remembered correctly. Lawrence's companions this afternoon were Mexicans, but they looked like rough customers who would know which end of the gun the bullets came out of.

All five were arrayed along the top of a sheer bluff that overhung the road to the old mine. All five lay belly-down. They looked bored. Two of them had squirmed close together so they were lying side by side and were, incredibly enough, smoking. Either they did not know that smoke from those dark little cigarillos would give them away, or quite possibly they simply did not care.

Being paid by the day instead of by the dead body, Matt thought just a little contemptuously. Then he corrected himself. Those men were possibly brave fighters who just happened to be bored stiff by the inactivity of lying too long in this ambush. He shouldn't judge them until he knew them.

While Matt watched, the two lay there with their heads close together, whispering like a pair of schoolboys hiding a prank from the teacher.

For a moment that mental image made Matt smile. He had had his share of pranks and secrets when he was a kid. He remembered how wicked it had felt.

But then he sobered. It was no prank these Mexican gunmen hoped to complete. They lay here intent on cold-blooded murder. His murder. That was about as serious as things could get, and he should not let himself forget it.

Matt took his time, lying inside a narrow niche between two jagged boulders while he assessed the situation.

For their ambush Lawrence and his men had chosen a broad, shallow shelf some forty or fifty feet over the road. Anyone traveling on the road would have to pass directly underneath them. The drawback to their position was that in order to leave this shelf, they now would have to climb up the hillside to more or less level ground. There was no way down. And the only way up was exposed to fire from above. From where Matt now was.

That was to Matt's advantage. On the plus side for the ambushers was the sheer weight of numbers. Five rifles shooting from below could create havoc. Splinters of jagged rock chips and splatters of hot lead could cut a man to pieces.

Better, Matt thought, if he did not let this dance begin.

He placed his Winchester down very carefully so as to avoid making any noise, then cupped his hands in front of his mouth to diffuse the sound.

"You. Down there." All five of them stiffened at the sound of a voice from above and behind. "Hold still. Completely still."

Matt thought he heard some murmuring. Quite possibly someone translating his English for the others, he suspected. That was all right. He wanted each of them to know what was being said. He would like to get out of this without any gunfire if he possibly could.

"Do not turn around. Do what I say, exactly what I say, and you will live to see another day. Try to bring your guns around and you will die here this day." He gave them a moment for the translation into Spanish, then said, "Whatever money you were promised for this will do you no good if all it buys is your coffin." He paused again.

"I want to start with you on the left, on the side toward San Iba. Very, very carefully pick your rifle up. Use your left hand. Pick it up by the barrel. Slow now. You wouldn't want me to get excited and shoot you by mistake. That's right. Nice and slow, thank you. Now toss it. That's right. Just toss it out in front of you. Never mind where it falls. Just pitch it right out there. Thank you."

There was a loud clatter of metal and breaking wood when the carbine hit the road. That was one ruined Winchester, ruined or at the very least in bad need of a gunsmith's services.

"Now your pistols. Yes, I see that one you are lying on. That one too. Toss it, please. Thank you." The two revolvers were not as loud when they struck the road below, but the fall would have done them no good.

"Now you," Matt said, still not showing himself. "The next man in line. Toss your rifle, please. Thank you. Now that pistol. Yes, thanks. Now you."

The third man, the one who had placed himself in the middle either for protection or because he wanted to be able to more easily issue orders, was the American gunman called Lawrence. Lawrence did not look happy, not even a little bit.

"Who are you?" he remembered. "Where are you?"

"You know darn good and well who I am and never mind where I am at the moment. Just do what I say and you'll live to see the sun come up tomorrow. Otherwise you'll be dead and buried long before then."

"You're a coward," he accused. "Show yourself and face me like a man."

Matt almost smiled at that. "Face the three of you, d'you mean? I'm not quite that dumb. Now toss that rifle like I told you."

"And if I don't?" Lawrence's voice was loud and his words defiant, but Matt suspected the man felt a need to put on a bold show before these Mexican underlings.

"If you don't you will not live to taste one more drink or kiss one more señorita. You saw me when your friend Curly tried to take me. Are you any faster or do you shoot straighter than he did?"

There was no immediate response. Matt added, "You're out of time, Lawrence. Make a play or throw that rifle down."

"This is no fair fight," Lawrence accused.

"You are absolutely right. It isn't. Now do whatever you choose. Or just lie there and let me shoot you. I suppose that could be considered a choice." There was no way Matt Bodine would shoot a man who presented no threat to him. But he doubted Lawrence would even understand such a reluctance; he certainly would have none if their positions were reversed and he was the one up on this hillside looking down with a gun in his hands.

Matt eased the hammer of his Winchester down silently, then held it out away from his body a few inches and very deliberately cocked it again so Lawrence could hear the sound of the action working.

"Don't . . . don't shoot." Lawrence was scowling when he pitched his own rifle into the void. But pitch it he did. The weapon made a most satisfying clatter on the rocks below.

Lawrence's revolver followed, and then the weapons on the remaining two armed Mexicans in short order.

"See?" Matt called down. "That was easy enough, wasn't it, and no one got hurt. Not you. Not me. I'd call that a pretty fair deal all the way around. Now if you gentlemen will excuse me, I have places to go and people to see."

Matt stood, touched the brim of his Stetson, and began the short climb to the ridge line that would take him back down to where his horse and mule were tied.

Somewhere not far ahead, he knew, he would find the place where Lawrence and these men had left their horses. It probably would be a good idea if he were to gather them up and take them along with him. He could turn them loose and eventually they would find their way home. In the meantime they would not help those five very unhappy ambushers get back to San Iba.

Matt was smiling when he thought of how tired those boys' feet would be when they got there.

Yessir, very likely the general store would have a run on the sale of Epsom salts tonight.

He sobered. Very likely there would be a run on firearms too to replace the guns Matt broke.

Still, he'd done everything he could to avoid bloodshed. If anyone wanted to push things beyond this, it would be on his own head not Matt's.

Of a sudden Matt was anxious to get back to camp and meet Sam there.

CHAPTER 30

When he reached the point where he should turn off the road and begin climbing into the mountains in order to reach Sam and their camp, Matt stopped for a few moments in thought.

He was leading the horses the five ambushers had ridden, and they presented something of a problem. If he turned them loose, they would inevitably find their way back to their respective homes. That was certain. It was also what he wanted.

The thing that worried him, though, was that the horses, herd creatures to the core, might very well follow him to the place where he and Sam had their camp before they wandered away and headed back to wherever their usual homes were. And once a horse has been to a place, it can easily and unerringly go back to it.

A vaquero who was wise to the ways of the horse could very well rely upon that trait in order to find Matt and Sam. A second attempted ambush might very well be more successful than the first had been. That was a risk the brothers would be willing to accept if and only if there was no other reasonable option.

After a few moments of thinking about this, Matt grinned. He dismounted long enough to lead the mule off the road and tie it. Not only was there no need to take it with him, it could become a liability if he did; he did not know how fast the little mule could run, and there was a distinct possibility that he would be in a rather large hurry after he got rid of the spare horses.

Leaving the mule hidden, he stepped back into his saddle and took up the lead rope.

A half hour later he rode straight into the mine where Sam and his Indian companions had been imprisoned in chains. There was no guard posted along the road, only the signs warning visitors away.

It was almost dark by then, the dusk lying heavy over the mountainside. Matt could not make out the Branvol homestead from here, but he thought he knew where it would be. He peered in that direction for a moment, his heart heavy with the thought that Anita's world and that of her children, both the boy and the as-yet-unborn child, would be shattered by the developments they found here.

Still, one needs to know the truth before one can come to terms with it. If Pete was dead it was better for her and the children that she know. Sam was right. They needed to find out.

Matt rode bold as brass into the yard outside the handful of old mine buildings.

Yellow lamplight streamed out of the windows of the largest building, and there was the enticing aroma of wood smoke and frying bacon in the air.

Before he could reach the corral where a pair of heavy draft horses picked at hay in a small bunk, a door creaked open and light spilled into the yard. A large man with a bamboo cane in his hands peered out. *"Quien es?"* he called. "Who's there?"

Matt drew rein and raised his hand to touch the brim of his Stetson. "Evenin', neighbor."

The big man stepped out into the yard. He was a tough-looking customer, Matt thought. Likely he was the one Sam had told him about. What was the name again? Oh, yes. Wilhelm, that was it. Case Wilhelm. Matt would've bet a dollar to a doughnut that this was Sam's tormentor Case Wilhelm.

"Who are you and what do you want here?" Wilhelm demanded.

"Neighbor, I'm just a delivery boy or so y' might say. Fella down the road stopped me and asked since I was going in this direction would I fetch these horses along with me. Said I was to leave them here."

"I'm not expecting any horses," Wilhelm said.

Matt shrugged. "It's no business of mine. I can just turn them loose if you like."

"Did this man say who he was or what the horses were for?"

"No, he didn't."

"It seems strange to me that someone would have five spare horses, all of them saddled and bridled but no riders for them."

"Yes, sir, I expect I'd agree with you. I wonder about it too, but it's no business of mine, and since I was heading this way anyhow, figured I could as easy do the man a favor. I meant no offense to you, though, and trust I've given none."

"No, uh, of course not. Here. Let me open the gate to the pen there. We'll put the horses in there with the others. You're welcome to put your animal in too. You can take a meal with us and spend the night if you like.

If you are a hand with that gun on your hip you might even find work here."

"I thank you for the offer of both the provender and the job, neighbor, but I'm bent on doing me some prospecting up in these hills. I got the fever upon me, you might say. And truth to tell, coming across your operation here is a heap of encouragement to me. Knowing you can make a living here from whatever it is you're mining . . . and understand, please, that I'm not asking questions, no, sir . . . but knowing you have a going mine, why, that encourages me no end, sir. Makes me awful glad that I happened to come this way. Now the one favor I might ask of you in return for fetching in these horses would be for you to tell me, please, does the road run on past here or have I come to the end of it?"

"There's no road past this point," Wilhelm reported.

"Then I'll thank you for that information, sir, and ride back a little way. I saw a path a few miles back that I think will get me up onto the mountain so I can do some looking around."

"Would you do me a favor?" Wilhelm asked.

"If I can, sure thing," Matt told him.

"This outfit hires prisoners to perform some of the labor, and some of them have escaped. If you see any raggedy-ass Indians lurking around, would you bring them in, please."

"Oh, I . . . I dunno if I could do such a thing as that. I don't have any authority to arrest anybody, you understand. And it isn't the sort of thing. . . ." Matt's voice tailed away. Then after a moment he smiled and said, "But I could come tell you if I see any. Would that help?"

"Yeah. Yeah, mister, that would help a lot. In fact, I'd pay a reward to you for information like that."

"Oh, I don't know as I'd want a reward, but I'd appreciate a little grub maybe."

"Look, are you sure you won't come in and eat with us? You'd be welcome to."

"Thank you, but I get uncomfortable with a lot of folks around. I'm what you might call shy," Matt lied, inside himself feeling like breaking up laughing.

"Fine, but keep your eyes open for escaped prisoners while you're searching for mineral. I would appreciate it."

"I'll do that, friend."

Wilhelm stepped near and extended a hand up to Matt, who was still in his saddle. The big man introduced himself, not knowing that Matt already knew good and well who he was. "And your name would be . . . ?"

"Tam," Matt said. "Tam O'Shanter."

Wilhelm stepped back and frowned. "It seems I've heard that name before, though I can't recall where."

Matt was about to choke to keep himself from bursting out in guffaws. Tam O'Shanter indeed. "You might could have heard it, Mr. Wilhelm," he said solemnly. "I have cousins who go by the same name."

"Yes, well, I'm sure we've not met before. I would remember if we had."

"So would I," Matt said cheerfully. "But I expect we might meet again sometime."

"Come by any time, Tam," Wilhelm said. "Any time."

Matt touched the brim of his Stetson and politely backed the bay a few steps before he wheeled it around and headed down the road at a lope.

He forced himself to wait until he had a good solid mile behind him before he burst out laughing. Tam O'Shanter, was it? Sam was going to like that. Matt was sure of it.

CHAPTER 31

Sam listened closely and frowned. Someone was coming. Two horses. He could think of no one Matt would bring here to their camp, so it could be that the horses belonged to someone from the prison mine down below. As a precaution Sam tugged the blanket higher over the sleeping Apache girl and slipped into the darkness away from the fire, Winchester in hand.

A few minutes later he was able to relax. The sounds were made by Matt's horse and by a pack animal trailing behind it.

On a whim, Sam remained in the shadows while Matt dismounted and tied both animals on the picket rope where Sam's horse was. Matt removed the panniers from the back of the little pack mule and unsaddled his bay, then gave horse and mule a quick rubdown.

While he worked with the curry comb, Matt spoke to the form lying beside the tiny fire. "You could get up and give me a hand here, you know," Matt said to the sleeping girl. "Don't think a couple days in prison gives you an excuse to laze about while I wait on you. Keep this up and I'll make you go get your own food. I'll be eating bacon and biscuits. You can scrounge up some nuts and berries. Or grass maybe. D'you fancy a bowl of grass stems or do you like the buds better? Just don't expect to reap the rewards if I have to do all the work for you."

Matt's tone turned serious. "Say now, you aren't coming down sick or something like that, are you? Do you want me to mix you up one of my mama's poultices or a tonic maybe? Are you all right, Sam? Dagnabbit, don't just lay there. Talk to me."

Matt set the curry comb aside and strode to the mound of blankets by the fire. He obviously saw the spill of raven hair peeping out at the top, but not the person that hair belonged to.

Sam came forward then, moving silent as a ghost just behind Matt.

Matt leaned down and pulled the blanket back, exposing the face and shoulders not of his brother, but of a young woman he'd never seen before.

"Boo," Sam whispered, practically in Matt's ear.

Matt jumped and let out a loud yip. And that brought the girl out of her slumber. She sprang to her knees, fear in her eyes but determination in the set of her jaw . . . and a wicked little knife clutched in her fist.

"Whoa! Wait a minute," Sam said. "Everybody calm down. I'm sorry. Really."

"Who . . . ?"

"What's . . . ?"

Sam took Matt by the elbow and pulled him away, then knelt beside the girl and placed a hand very lightly on her wrist to push the knife down.

"Matt, this is Willow Buds Pale in Springtime. But you can call her Willow. Willow, this is my brother Matt, the one I was telling you about. I, uh, I'm sorry if my little joke went awry."

The girl sat up and tugged at her clothes to smooth and straighten everything. Somehow in the process of her doing that, the little knife disappeared.

"No, don't get up," Sam said. "I want you to stay down, please. And pull the blanket up high. You need to stay warm. Matt, did you bring anything we can use to make a good rich broth or a soup? Willow was struck by a snake this afternoon. A rattler. I know some of the venom got into her bloodstream for I wasn't able to get to it quickly. She hasn't been eating much lately so she needs nourishment more than anything else. And she needs to lie quiet."

Cold sweat beaded on Willow's upper lip and across her forehead. Sam used his bandanna to mop it away, then tucked the blanket tight around her shoulders and high under her chin.

"We have tinned milk," Matt said, "and dried beef. That and some saleratus and flour will make a nice thick gravy to put over some of your biscuits." He smiled at the pretty girl. "Grub like that would make anybody feel perky."

"Before you go making even more of a fool of yourself than you usually do, brother, you might want to know that Willow's husband is a friend of mine. We were both in chains down there, he and I. He befriended and helped me."

"She. . . . Oh!" Matt gave the girl a sheepish little-boy look. "I'm sorry, miss. Uh, ma'am, I mean. Sorry."

"Lie quiet, Willow. We'll have a proper meal for you shortly."

Sam and Matt turned to the mundane and long-familiar chores of putting a campfire meal together, something they had been doing for almost as long as either could remember. Soon they had a fresh pot of coffee boiling while a pan of biscuits browned and, in a can that was pressed into service as a pot, Sam's chipped-beef concoction bubbled.

Willow was able to eat very little and soon she was asleep, her frail body striving to fight off the effects of the poison from the snakebite. The brothers tended to her first, then when she was asleep, filled plates for themselves and carried them a short distance away from the fire, both to keep out of the light in case some of Jarold Williams's men should happen on them and to avoid disturbing the sleeping girl.

"Now," Sam said. "Tell me about your day; then I will fill you in on mine."

CHAPTER 32

The blood brothers fell quickly into a pattern. Sleeping during the day, at night they crept down to the mine, where Matt kept watch with his rifle at hand in case Sam should be discovered. Sam, meanwhile, slipped cautiously down onto the loose-tailings slope where the crushed ore from the mine was discarded.

Working silently lest his presence be betrayed to the men above, Sam dug through the tailings in search of Peter Branvol's body.

"The really unpleasant thing," Sam said one morning after an exhausting night of labor and stealth, "is that not finding anything proves nothing. Am I not finding Pete because his body is not there? Or am I simply not finding him yet?" Sam sighed. "Under these circumstances I hate to admit it, but my professors back in school were correct. It is just awfully hard to prove a negative. In a situation like this a negative offers neither comfort nor proof."

"Do you think we should quit?" Matt asked.

Sam shook his head. "Not yet. I'm beginning to get a feel for the way the discarded ore is distributed. And . . .

I hate to tell you this . . . but I am unfortunately finding something. Just not, well, not what we are looking for."

"Bodies?" Matt asked.

"Yes. Two who appear to have been prisoners, either Apache or Yaqui, and one middle-aged Mexican. I also found . . . Matt, I can't even decide if this last one was human remains or bones tossed down with kitchen leavings."

"This is bothering you," Matt said. "I'm sorry, Sam. Look, maybe it would help to take a night off and just sleep. Or I can dig."

"No." Sam smiled. "You would make such a racket the men at the mine would be sure to hear." He sobered. "Or the prisoners would."

The authorities in San Iba were already sending in new prisoners—victims really—to replace those who had escaped. There were five unfortunates living in the old mine adit now and laboring under the threat of whip and chain throughout the day.

As before, all of these new prisoners were Indians. None of the local Mexican population was ever sentenced to work at the mine, it seemed.

"What about a night off then? This is bothering you, Sam. I can see that it is."

"I just want to get it behind us so we can get away from here. Besides, I think I must be close. If I have any hope of finding out if Pete is down there, I think I'll do it soon. Give me two more nights. If I do not find him by then, we will just have to conclude that we are wrong about all this and go back to the ranch."

"Two nights. Fair enough. We should be about out of supplies by then anyway so that works out well enough. I'll take the mule back to Doc's livery and we can go out to the ranch."

"Speaking of which, I am hungry enough that I could eat that mule. What do you say we go see what Willow has cooked for our breakfast."

The young Apache woman had recovered sufficiently to begin performing most of their camp tasks. She still seemed weak, but by now it was apparent that the rattlesnake's venom would have no lasting ill effects on her.

The brothers made their way to their camp, which they had taken pains to hide and to improve over the last few days, to find a skillet of diced potatoes along with some sort of root and unidentifiable meat set at the side of some nearly cold coals at the fire pit.

"So where is your girlfriend?" Matt asked.

"She is a married woman, not one of your ladies fair," Sam protested.

"Fine. She could be one of the Queen of England's ladies-in-waiting for all I care. My question was, where the heck is she?"

Sam hunkered down beside the remains of their fire and felt of the skillet. There was very little residual heat in the heavy cast iron. "If I had to guess, Matt, I would say Willow decided the time was right for her to go home. I think she has gone to find her husband and her people."

"Without saying good-bye?"

"I could be wrong, but I think so, yes," Sam said.

"You Indians sure aren't very demonstrative, are you?"

"That is one of the first things they teach us," Sam said. "Never let a white man know what you are thinking."

"And mighty good you are at it too."

"Thank you," Sam said cheerfully.

"But I still think she could have said good-bye."

"I am just glad we were able to help. And look at the bright side, Matt. With only two of us sharing this, um, whatever it is"—he looked into the skillet and made a sour face—"there is more for each. Yum-yum."

"Fine. Now let's eat and get some sleep before the day turns too hot for comfort." Matt dug their utensils out and handed Sam a spoon. The two of them would eat out of the skillet rather than soil plates that would just have to be cleaned afterward.

"You're cutting things awful close, aren't you," Matt declared on the morning after the fourth night. "It's already too bright for comfort. The sun will be up in a few minutes." Matt paused. "Something is wrong, isn't there."

"Nothing more than what we already suspected, but yes. I found Pete's body. I was trying to work it free from the rocks, but it's awfully hard to do and remain quiet. I didn't want to alert anyone up above. It . . . he . . . isn't very far down the slope. I was afraid someone might hear."

"Tomorrow night then. We'll have to come back tomorrow night."

Sam nodded. "There is something else, Matt."

"Yes?"

"Something neither one of us thought of although we should have."

"Is it something we can handle?"

"Yes, of course, but . . . the body, Matt. It isn't in very good shape. It is hot down here and things, well, things decompose rather quickly. And then there are the things that live in the rocks. Mice, rats, I don't know what all is down there, but . . . it is not a very pretty sight, Matt. It could be we should just leave him there."

"No," Matt said emphatically. "We have to take him back. You haven't met Anita yet, but I can tell you that she will want to bury Pete even if she has to come back and find him herself."

"She wouldn't do such a thing as that surely."

"I think she might once she knows for sure that he is dead. We would have to tell her that much. And how we know for sure. And that would mean telling her where Pete's body is. You know we would even if we didn't want to. It would cause no end of trouble and there's no telling what those men might do if Anita came along and threatened to expose their secrets."

"The mine is no secret."

"No, but the murders are, and they've murdered more than just those Indians, bad as that is. Maybe the folks around here wouldn't say too much about some Apaches and Yaquis being killed out here, but they would sure squawk once they know that Americans and Mexicans have been murdered by these people. I really think Anita would be in danger of her life if she came and tried to claim Pete's body. Being a woman wouldn't be enough to protect her."

"But the condition of his body . . . you haven't seen it, brother."

"Fine. So we'll do something to cope with that. We can sew him into . . . I don't know. Yes, by gum, I do know. I'll take the blankets out of my bedroll. We can wrap him inside the canvas and tie him up nice and tight there. We've about used up our supplies, so there isn't much of a load for the mule to carry. We can wrap Pete up and pack him out on the mule. Anita doesn't ever have to see the condition he's in."

"She will insist on seeing him if only to know in her heart that it is Pete and that he is dead," Sam said.

"You're probably right about that, and there won't be

anything you or me can do to stop her, but we can try. After that"—he shrugged—"we can only do so much."

"Tonight," Sam said. "We will get a good sleep today and tonight I need you to come with me. It will take both of us to finish getting the body out of those stones and up to the road so we can load it onto the mule. The sensible thing from there, I think, will be for us to go down this evening already prepared to leave. As soon as we have Pete's body, we can pull out and head for the ranch. With any kind of luck we should be there by midday tomorrow."

"Good enough," Matt said. "Now move your elbow a little. You're blocking me from getting at that skillet, brother."

"The stuff tastes better than it looks, doesn't it," Sam agreed.

The two finished their meal, tidied up the campsite, and stretched out in their bedrolls to sleep.

When they woke up they were facing the muzzles of four very-large-caliber muskets.

CHAPTER 33

The Mexican soldiers wore tall hats with huge brass medallions on them and shiny brims, dark blue coats with brass buttons and the peculiar white canvas webbing crisscrossing their chests, with another brass medallion at the point where the stark white bands crossed. Sam always thought of those as being good aiming points. But then what did he know about military things; he was only an Indian.

Polished black leather accoutrements dangled from the webbing on the soldiers' uniforms. And, ominously enough, there were very long, very sharply pointed bayonets affixed to the muskets.

"Why are these bell boys here?" Matt asked.

Sam glanced toward Matt and gave his blood brother a half smile, then returned his attention to the Mexicans. "What can we do for you?" he asked the soldiers.

One of the men, presumably their leader although he wore no signs of superior rank that Matt could see, spoke to them. In Spanish.

Matt shook his head. "Sorry. I don't understand."

"No, um, no habba," Sam said.

"What the devil was that?"

"I told him we don't understand."

"You did?"

"I think I did," Sam said. "Maybe."

"You *think* so? Do me a favor, brother. Don't go saying any more stuff that you aren't sure of. You might could tell them to shoot us and never know you'd said it."

"Do any of you speak English?" Sam said to their captors. The response from the Mexicans was silence. The leader, however, did motion with his bayonet, prompting the brothers to their feet.

"I'm not real sure that I like this," Matt said.

"Local custom," Sam told him. "They're just trying to make us feel welcome."

"Hey, I believe that too." Matt smiled at his blood brother. "Sure I do."

The smile or perhaps the conversation did not set well with one of the soldiers. The man barked out an order, although neither brother had the least inkling of its meaning, and jabbed Matt in the belly with his bayonet.

"Hey!"

Sam bristled and was tempted to have at their captors. He probably would have gone for his Colt, never mind that there were four rifles cocked and aimed his way, except his gun belt was rolled and lying on the blanket where he had been sleeping until these soldiers showed up.

"Back off," Matt murmured.

"Are you all right?"

"Bruised maybe, but it didn't break the skin. Hurts like the very devil, though."

"They have four shots, Matt. And if those bayonets haven't been sharpened. . . ."

The Mexican who was giving the orders gave some more. Louder this time since his first instructions had not been obeyed. Then he gestured to indicate Matt and Sam should turn around. The hand motions they understood well enough even if the language was not shared. Reluctantly they turned around.

There were more orders given, the leader's voice loud and hard, and the shuffling of feet, the clatter of wood on metal as something was done with the muskets. Then rough hands grabbed hold of the brothers' arms from behind.

Matt had thoughts of a military-style execution by firing squad, and he would have been willing to bet that Sam did too. He resisted the tug on his arms as the soldier behind him tried to pull Matt's wrists behind his back.

If he only had his revolver. . . . But of course he did not. The best he would be able to do was to whirl around and try to overcome the soldiers before they could bring those long-barreled muskets to bear.

There was the sound of more scuffling on the loose gravel that covered the ground here, and then the loud, flat, ugly bellow of a large-caliber musket discharging.

Matt's heart turned to stone. He felt as if he had been suddenly stabbed through his heart. Sam! They'd shot Sam.

Matt whirled, right fist cocked, left hand groping for something or someone to fend off.

He stopped. Stood upright. His mouth gaped open in sheer astonishment.

All four Mexicans were on the ground. Sam was standing there unharmed.

And eight or . . . no, seven, there were seven . . . Apache warriors stood over the fallen Mexicans.

The soldiers looked considerably the worse for wear. Their fancy shakos with the glittering brass lay in the dust and their rifles were now in the hands of the Apaches. One of the soldiers, the one who had been the leader, was dying. His throat had been slashed so deeply it was a wonder his head remained on his shoulders, and blood gushed and gurgled out of the gaping cut in his throat.

The other three Mexicans were terrified.

They had every reason to be.

While Matt watched in openmouthed astonishment, an Apache warrior took one of the soldiers' own muskets and drove the bayonet socket-deep into a Mexican's chest. The soldier fell, either already dead or mercifully passed out. The Apache contemptuously tossed the rifle butt aside. The bayonet was still stuck deep in the soldier's chest so that the musket wobbled and then stood partially upright, moving very slightly with the attempts by the dying man to gasp for breath.

The remaining two soldiers turned and, much too late, tried to flee. Pairs of strong hands grabbed them. Bore them to the ground. Held them there while cold-faced Apache warriors slashed the scalps from the still-living Mexicans.

The soldiers were oddly silent while this was done. In deep shock was Matt's guess. They were so quiet that he could easily hear the slightly gritty sound of knife blades slicing through tough skin and grating on bone when the scalps were harvested.

When they were done with the scalping, the Apaches stood and one of them spit on the weeping soldier who lay at his feet looking up at his own scalp dangling from the hand of the dark warrior.

That Apache, who seemed to be the leader, said something in his own tongue and the others laughed.

Incredibly enough, at least to Matt's way of thinking, the Apaches paid no more attention to the soldiers, not to the dead nor to the pair who still lived despite having their scalps taken.

The Apaches turned then and gave their attention to Matt, and mostly to Sam.

The leader smiled. And stepped forward to greet Sam with a clasping of forearm to forearm. "It is good, Two Wolf. I see that you are well. This is the brother you speak of?"

"Yes. This one is my brother. It is a shame he did not get my good looks, is it not?"

Three of the Apaches laughed immediately. The others did so after one of the English-speaking warriors translated Sam's words for them.

"This is Matt," Sam announced. "Brother, these are my friends Koronado and Nana and Tomas." He pointed. "These men I do not yet know." To the Apaches he added, "We owe each of you a debt of thanks."

Matt noticed that the Mexican with the musket planted in his chest had ceased breathing. The two who had been scalped lay silent. He guessed they were pretending to be dead so they would not draw any more attention to themselves.

The Apaches had not forgotten about them, however. Several of the warriors took the trembling Mexicans by the arms and dragged them away. Wherever they were being taken, and for whatever purpose, Matt was awfully glad he was not going with them. He had heard about the terrible things the Apaches did to captive enemies.

A few moments later several others came out of the brush in ghostlike silence. Women and a gaggle of children of various ages. The children divided their wide-eyed stares between the dead Mexicans and the live visitors.

Then, from not far away, the screaming began. The scalped but living Mexicans were probably wishing by now that they could exchange places with these two who were already dead and beyond all pain.

Sam seemed to pay no attention to the horrible sounds. He came toward Matt with the leader of the Apaches and a young, rather pretty Apache woman.

"Brother, I'd like you to meet my friend Koronado, and you already know his wife Willow."

Somewhere close by the Mexicans were screaming, their voices already hoarse. The children tore their attention away from the Cheyenne and American visitors and scampered away to watch the much more interesting entertainment offered by the soldiers.

CHAPTER 34

"Are we having a celebration here?" Matt asked an hour or so later.

"It looks like some of us are." Sam nodded toward the Apache women, all of whom were kneeling around a metate chattering like so many magpies while their hands combined to make the work light and cheerful. The children were off to the side playing quietly at games Matt could not begin to understand. The men, once they'd finished with the Mexicans, had gathered up their newfound wealth of muskets and disappeared into the brush on the mountain slopes.

Sam raised his voice and called, "Willow, may we ask what you ladies are doing over there?"

"We prepare to cook. You see? Corn cakes. Soon our men will return with meat."

Matt shuddered to think just what kind of meat they might bring back should the Apache men run into another patrol of Mexican soldiers. Not that he suspected the tribe of being cannibals. They clearly were not. But all that screaming while the soldiers died so terribly and so slowly was not exactly something Matt wanted to hear at mealtime. Or for that matter at any time of day or night. He'd had about all he really wanted of it.

"Do you know when they will be back?" Matt asked. The thought of food was usually enough to stir his hunger, and now he had the sight of those women grinding corn to reinforce that.

"Soon," Willow said, her voice light and cheerful now that she was reunited with her husband. She seemed almost to have forgotten about the snakebite, although she did continue to favor that arm a little.

Matt heard Sam chuckling beside him, and turned to ask, "What're you laughing about?"

"Nothing really. Just realizing that 'soon' to an Apache is probably the same as 'soon' to a Cheyenne."

"Oh," Matt said dispiritedly. He knew quite good and well that in his adopted tribe "soon" could mean anything from five minutes to five weeks. Or five months, for that matter. It was anything but the same as the concept of "soon" to an American.

As it turned out, they did not have terribly long to wait. Within an hour the Apache warriors materialized out of the scrub with the same ghostlike silence with which they left. They were carrying poles from which dangled a fat doe and a half-grown fawn. No gunshots had been heard, so the deer may well have been harvested far from camp. It was also possible that a trick in the shape of the gullies and washes on the mountainside had contained the sounds or directed the noise elsewhere. The important thing was that if the shots were not heard at the camp, it was most unlikely that they had been heard down below at the mine where Case Wilhelm and his men were.

The deer were quickly skinned and the fawn plastered with mud, then buried on top of a bed of coals with more glowing coals added on top of it. The meat would take hours to cook, but when it was done it would be moist and tender. A layer of loose dirt was spread over the buried meat and a hot, smokeless fire was quickly built on top of that.

The doe was cut into strips that were piled on a broad, tightly woven tray. First the men, then the women, and finally the children would be allowed to select whatever strips they pleased and hold them over the fire on long sticks.

"Come. Eat now," Koronado offered with a wave of his hand.

"I won't be slow about it," Matt said. "Are you coming, Sam?"

"Right with you, brother."

Koronado provided each guest with a long stick and gave them the honor of choosing the first strips of dark red meat. After those, however, it would be every man for himself.

Sam did not show anything in his expression, but he found it amusing that this camp where he and Matt had been for the past several days was now inexplicably the property of Koronado's band of Apaches. Not that it mattered, of course. The earth is the property of the Great Spirit and not any individual human.

In his heart Sam still held many of the beliefs of his Cheyenne people. He had been given a good education by his mother, by Matt's family, and later on when he attended the white men's schools, and he considered himself a good Christian. But he still equated God with the Great Spirit he had known since infancy. It was something he had long since accepted and no longer bothered trying to rationalize.

"Do you have whiskey?" Koronado asked while the brothers dangled strips of sizzling venison over the fire.

"No. Sorry."

Koronado grinned. "No matter. We will use these guns. Go steal some."

"Where will you do this?" Sam asked, suddenly interested.

"There." Koronado pointed down at the mine from which he and Sam so recently escaped. "Those men are bad. They should die." The grin returned. "They have whiskey. I smell it on the stink of their breath each morning."

"You will kill them?"

"Of course."

"Would you mind telling us when you will do this thing?"

Koronado gave Sam a hard look. "Why you want to know this?"

"Because my brother and I have something we must do down on that slope below the arrastra. It will cause noise. Perhaps much noise. If we do what we must do when you and your warriors are raiding the white men's place, it will be of help to us. They will be too busy with you to think about any sound we make."

"Ah. *Bueno.*"

"What?"

"Good. Means good. It is well."

"Yes, friend, it is good. Whenever you and your warriors are ready, we will all go down together and each will do those things that must be done."

Later, their bellies full to groaning with broiled venison and rough-ground corn cakes, Matt leaned close to Sam and whispered, "You were mighty careful to avoid telling Koronado just what it is we have t' do down there. How's come?"

"Because, my ignorant brother, with most tribes it is taboo, a truly terrible thing, to have anything to do with the dead. I do not know about the Apaches in particular, but most tribes would be scandalized by the idea of digging up a body and hauling it off. They could be so upset as to refuse to help us or even try to stop us. It's better, I think, to say nothing on the subject."

"All right. In that case I reckon I can mind my mouth for the next few hours." Matt belched loudly. Then he sat up straighter and smiled. "Say now. With that outa the way, I think I can hold one more strip o' that good meat."

There was still a fair amount left, even after the children were allowed at it. Matt groaned aloud when he leaned forward to pick up a strip and spear it on the end of his roasting stick, but pick it up he did.

"Matt, if you bust wide open, don't look for me to help you."

"It's a chance I'm willing to take, brother."

CHAPTER 35

The brothers rode in almost complete silence for the first hours of their journey off the mountainside and down to the Branvol ranch. They were sobered, and in some respects saddened, by the screams and gunfire they'd heard coming from the mine while they were busy securing Pete's decomposing body and carrying it up to the waiting mule and horses.

The tarpaulin that originally served Matt as a bedroll cover worked just as well as a shroud, but it had been distasteful work even so.

Once the body was inside the tarp with rope lashings all around, it was heavy work to get it up the steep slope of loose, slippery rock, but between them they had managed.

"Thank you," Sam said when the task was finally done and the body was loaded onto the patient little mule. "I could not have done this by myself."

Matt did not answer. He was no stranger to death. Far from it. But Pete's murder hit him particularly hard. Pete had been a friend. And young. He had left behind a lovely young widow and a fine son, with another child on the way. That was ugly. All the more so because the murderers knew about Pete's family.

At the same time, both brothers found sobering the distinctive scent of burnt gunpowder in the air and the sharper, far uglier stink of blood and excreta from the carnage on the level above.

"I don't want to go up and look," Matt muttered when they were done loading the mule.

"No," Sam agreed. "No point."

Matt looked at his brother, but as always in situations like this, Sam's face was impassive. Matt could not tell if Sam was unaffected by the slaughter that had taken place up there or if it actually pleased him.

It was not until hours later when they were within a few miles of the Branvol homestead that Matt came out with it and asked the question.

"To tell you the truth, my brother, my thoughts were selfish ones," Sam replied.

"Selfish? Whatever could you mean by that?"

"While the Apache were back there at the mine doing the things that needed to be done to punish those whites for their crimes, all I could think about was that Koronado or some of his band were doing the thing that I vowed I would do."

"I don't understand."

"When that man Wilhelm was beating me with that bamboo flail that he seemed to love so much, Matt, I made a vow. I promised myself that I would one day face Wilhelm man-to-man and make him regret the things he did to me. And to so many others before me. Now . . . that is a pleasure that was granted to Koronado instead of to me."

"Then perhaps there is a reason why that was so," Matt offered.

"I could have taken him. You met him. You know."

"I do know, brother, and I agree that you could have taken him in any sort of fight or contest. I also know that revenge is a strange thing. It's a two-edged sword and it can cut with both sides. Could be that seeking revenge woulda done more to hurt you than it did him."

"Are you saying . . . ?"

"Don't get riled, Sam. I'm just saying maybe there's reasons for things that you and me don't always know about. All we can do is the best we can. Do our best at what we think is right an' let it go."

Sam sighed. "You are right." Then his dark features split into a broad, uncomplicated grin. "Which only tells me that there has to be a first time for everything."

"Yeah, now tell me the one about how even a blind pig finds an acorn every once in a while."

Sam sobered, his face becoming impassive. "I don't think I know that story, Matt. Tell it to me, please."

Matt laughed. "Come on, idiot. Pete's place . . . oh! I guess I mean t' say Anita's place, is right over yonder and I don't want t' ride into that yard laughing an' us pulling Pete's body along with us."

"No. This time I am very sorry to say that you are right again, my brother."

They rode the last few hundred yards in silence. Matt felt comfortable enough there to dismount without waiting for an invitation, but Sam stayed in the saddle. It was he who held the lead rope to the mule carrying the body in its impromptu shroud.

Anita must have heard them ride in. She came to the door, a dish towel in her hand, and smiled when she saw Matt. "You are back. Good. I wondered where you had gotten to. And this would be the brother who I heard so much about?"

"That's right, ma'am. This is Sam."

"It is a pleasure to meet you, Sam. Pete told me much about both of you." She started forward with her hand extended in welcome, but stopped short when she saw the shape of the burden on the back of the little Spanish mule.

Anita's hand flew to her mouth and her eyes grew wide in sudden pain and horror. "No. Oh . . . *no!*"

She whirled and raced back inside the house, slamming the door closed as if that would shut out the ugly reality that had fallen upon her.

Matt turned his back to the house of anguish and snatched his hat off in frustration.

"Well," Sam said. "I think that went well, did it not?"

Matt looked mutely up at his brother, then shrugged and motioned for Sam to get down. After all, it was obvious that Anita was not feeling up to the regular social conventions at the moment.

"I figure," Matt said, "we can store the body just like it is. I haven't looked around all that much, but maybe there's a springhouse that would stay cool. If not"—he shrugged—"we'll put Pete in a shed or something."

"Where we should put Peter is into the ground," Sam said.

"Yeah, I know, but it's been so long already that another day or two isn't gonna make all that much difference. Anita is Catholic. That's one of the things she mentioned while I was here, how proud an' happy her family was when Pete converted to the Church.

"You can't go into town, of course. You might be recognized there, but I'm still all right with the folks in San Iba, I think. I can go in and get the priest. Bring him back here for the burying. I think that would be safer than taking Pete to the church. After all, nobody is supposed t' know about any of this."

Sam nodded. "That would be sensible, yes." Straight-faced, he added, "It is most unlike you, Matt, to be sensible."

"Yeah, well, even a blind pig finds an acorn . . . say, stop me if you've heard this story before."

"No, please go on, I am most anxious to hear this story you continue to speak of. It must be exciting."

If Anita had not been inside grieving and probably trying to comfort a little boy who suddenly had no daddy, Matt would have jumped on Sam and wrestled him. Or tried to. As it was, that sort of horseplay would have to wait.

"You can take care of things here, Sam. Help me get Pete settled someplace out of the sun; then I'll ride to San Iba for the priest."

"When you do," Sam said, "you might remember to tell them about the massacre at the mine. You could say that you were prospecting nearby and heard gunfire and screams, but you were too frightened to go see what happened there."

"Good idea. And I dang sure did hear some ugly noises coming from there. I'll do that. Otherwise, there's no telling how long it will take for the bodies to be found and properly buried. But I think I won't mention any of that until I already have the priest started on his way out here. We wouldn't want him lured away by the prospect of superior numbers."

"Are you suggesting that a priest might be greedy, Matt?"

"Not at all." Matt took the lead rope from Sam and began leading the mule toward the ranch outbuildings to find a spot where they could stash Pete. "Actually I was gonna use that comment as an illustration."

"About . . . ?"

"Blind pigs, Sam. And acorns. Just wait until you hear this one. You're gonna love it."

The brothers continued to prattle nonsense back and forth while they conducted a brief search of the available spots, looking for someplace that would be shaded and relatively cool. Eventually they settled for putting Pete's body in a zinc-lined grain bin. It might or might not stay cool there, but at least it would be safe from rats.

"Go on now, Matt. Go get that priest. I'll just wait on the porch while the lady and her boy adjust to losing Pete."

"Right." Matt picked up the mule's lead rope—they would not be needing the long-eared creature again so he might as well return it to the livery while he was in town—then mounted his horse and turned it toward the road.

This was turning out to be a long day. And a hard one.

CHAPTER 36

Matt was just about worn down to a nub by the time he reached San Iba and Doc Tippett's livery. The day was late and the miles many, but he still had a long way to go. He turned the little mule into the corral and went back into the barn to find Doc.

"Sorry to bother you, but I was wondering, could I leave my horse here for a few days and take a fresh mount while it's resting up? At your regular rates, of course."

"Take your pick, son. And there won't be any charge for the use of the horse." The old man grinned. "It was worth it to me to see the look on Lawrence's face when he and those Mexicans of his came dragging back into town looking madder than an entire flock of wet hens. If I was you, Matt, I'd stay clear of Lawrence from now on."

"Thanks for the advice, Doc. I'll be sure an' take it if the choice is left up to me."

Matt switched his saddle to a likely-looking paint that hadn't been in Doc's corral the last time he was here. The horse was not tall, but it had a broad chest with the forelegs set well apart and good hindquarters. It was no beauty, with a ratty tail and pencil neck, but it was not looks that Matt wanted.

He shook hands with Doc and headed out into the gathering dusk, hoping he could catch the priest at the little church down at the Mexican end of town. He was halfway there when he heard a loud voice call out, "Tam." It meant nothing to him until the speaker added, "Hey, there. O'Shanter."

Oh, yes. That silliness out at the mine. He had given that name to Case Wilhelm when he took the ambush party's horses there.

But Wilhelm was dead now. Wasn't he?

Matt reined the paint to a halt. He could see the form of the man who called out to him, but he was standing in shadow and it took Matt a moment to realize that it was indeed Wilhelm. The man must not have been at the mine when Koronado's Apaches struck. That was news Sam would be interested in.

"Howdy," Matt said cheerfully. He had to wonder, though, if the jig was up about his little joke with the name. "How're you this fine evening, Wilhelm."

It was not until the name was already out of his mouth that Matt realized he could not remember if Wilhelm had introduced himself out there or if this was knowledge he was not supposed to have. No, the man had been friendly. He had given Matt his name. Hadn't he?

Wilhelm stepped out from under the overhang along the sidewalk and came toward the paint. "I heard you had a little run-in with some friends of mine."

"Were they your friends? I wish I'd known that," Matt said. "We might have gotten along a little better if I had."

"That could be," Wilhelm said. "Mention it to them the next time you see them."

"I will. If there's a next time."

"Lawrence tells me there will definitely be a next time."

"Really? Face-to-face? By himself, with no gang of riflemen to do the shooting for him? Somehow, Mr. Wilhelm, I don't think that is something I have to worry about."

"I heard that, you son of a bitch." The voice came from just inside the doorway of the building where Wilhelm had been standing. A man came out onto the sidewalk. Lawrence. He looked mad enough to spit.

"Are you sure you want to call me that, mister?" Matt asked.

"I'm sure. I'm also calling you a coward. Sneaking up on us like you done, that's a coward's way of doing."

Matt laughed. "Let me see if I got this straight. You and your friends lay an ambush for me, five of you to one, then when I turn the tables, I am the one who's a coward while you and your boys are the wronged parties. Is that the way you see it?"

"Well, uh. . . ."

Matt stepped down from the paint and dropped the reins. He did not know if the horse would ground-tie, but if it ran off now he would just have to look for it at the barn later. Right at this moment he had other things to think about.

"Is that the way you see it, Lawrence?" Matt repeated. "I already know you're a back-shooter and a sneak, but are you a coward too?"

"I . . . I . . . ," Lawrence sputtered. He did not seem to very much like the situation he found himself in now. Obviously he had been making some loud talk to his boss. But that was before Matt showed up to call his bluff. Now he had to go through with a fight one-on-one or back water.

"Maybe I . . . maybe I got things wrong," Lawrence said. "I can see how you might've, uh, *thought* we was wanting to ambush somebody. But that ain't it at all. We was, um, we was waiting for a deer to come down that road. They're known to do that, you know. We was out there hunting deer. But I can see how you'd of misunderstood. There's, uh, no hard feelings now that I see how you come to make such a mistake."

"What if I have hard feelings?" Matt asked.

"Don't . . . don't . . . oh, Jesus!" Lawrence quickly unbuckled his gun belt and let it down onto the boards of the sidewalk. "Don't shoot me."

"Of course not," Matt said. "After all, nobody here has hard feelings. Isn't that right, Case? You, him, me, we none of us got hard feelings."

Wilhelm gave Lawrence a withering look that suggested the man was very quickly going to find himself unemployed in addition to being seen in town as a coward and a back-shooter.

"Is that right, Case?" Matt repeated. "There's no hard feelings by anybody."

"Yeah. That's for sure, Tam. That's for sure." He bent and picked up Lawrence's gun belt and draped it contemptuously over his shoulder. Lawrence made no effort to retrieve his weapon. The would-be gunman retreated back indoors as inconspicuously as he could. "Can I ask you something, Tam?" Wilhelm said.

"Go ahead, friend."

"I asked my boss about you."

"That would be Williams?"

"That's right. I work for Mr. Williams. He said he tried to hire you. There's an opening, you know. A couple of them maybe. Have you given his offer any thought? He pays real good."

"That's nice of you, Case. I thank you for thinking about me."

"Will you join us?"

"I reckon not, thanks."

"I kinda wish you'd change your mind about that, Tam. I sure would hate to see you and me on opposite sides of the fence. There's something you ought to know, though. That idiot Lawrence only thinks he's good with a gun. Me, I *am* as good as Lawrence thought he was. Guns, fists, knives, it don't matter to me. I can handle all of them, and as you can see I'm still walking upright. Nobody I've ever faced can say the same."

"Thank you for the warning, Case. I appreciate it."

"I meant that job offer, you know. I still do."

"I'll tell you something true, Case. I hope there's never need for the two of us to settle anything between us, but if we do, may the better man win and no regrets afterward."

Wilhelm grinned. "I like your style, Tam. Dang me for a fool if I don't."

"G'day, Case." Matt touched the brim of his Stetson, then swung back onto the paint. He still had to go find that priest and get him out to the Branvol place.

CHAPTER 37

Father Estevan did not own a horse. Did not have any English either, but at the moment that was the lesser of Matt's problems with the man. Through an English-speaking parishioner, the scrawny padre explained that he knew where he could borrow a burro if that would help.

"Well, no, I don't reckon it would." Matt sighed. "I'd hoped to get outa town without anybody knowing what I was doing here, but that might not be possible. Tell you what. I'll go back to Doc Tippett's livery and borrow another horse; then I'll come back here. Tell him to wait right here, please. I won't be long."

"*Sí, señor.* I will tell him." After a brief exchange the parishioner nodded and again turned to Matt. "He will be ready, Señor."

Matt felt like he was running a gantlet when he passed the length of the town, now in full darkness, but he saw no one who took any interest in him—at least no outward display of interest—and ran into neither Case Wilhelm nor the frustrated bullyboy named Lawrence. Matt was not sorry to have missed them.

He selected a docile, heavy-bodied gray for

Father Estevan to ride, and led it back through town to the church.

"Ready, Father?"

The parishioner had to translate even that. Not that Matt found that to be unreasonable. He would not have understood if the same very simple question had been asked of him in Spanish.

Matt helped the priest awkwardly into the saddle, then swung onto his rented paint.

It was well past dark when the two left the church, and Matt was on edge, his hand resting close to the grips of his Colt until they cleared the outskirts of San Iba and were on the road to the Branvol place.

"If you need to stop for any reason, Father, just . . . what am I asking you for anyhow? You don't understand a word I'm saying."

The little priest, who looked to be a man of fifty or so with more gray than black in his tonsure, smiled and nodded. Matt was sure he could have sung filthy drinking songs and the padre would have had the same outward response.

The priest was willing, though, even eager to go once he heard that he was needed to perform the rituals of the Church for a deceased parishioner. He was carrying a bundle containing his vestments and Bible, a tiny vial of holy water, and Matt could not begin to comprehend what else. The main thing from Matt's point of view was that Anita would be comforted. She badly needed that.

"I expect we'll be there before midnight," Matt rambled, wanting to make the priest comfortable with his tone of voice whether the actual words were understood or not. "I don't know how hard we can push these horses as I'm not familiar with either one of them. Doc Tippett says they're pretty good for rented horses. But then you know how rented horses are, don't you, Father?"

Father Estevan smiled and bobbed his head up and down. Matt was not entirely sure if that, however, was an effort to be agreeable or if it was simply in response to the motion of the gray.

"Tomorrow after we get through the burying, we can—"

A yellow rose of flame bloomed in the darkness on the uphill side of the road and an angry bumblebee droned rapidly past Matt's face.

Except the rose was a blossom of fire, a muzzle flash, and the "bee" was a heavy lead bullet zipping past.

Matt did not wait for explanations. He vacated the saddle and dashed into the brush on the roadside, leaving the paint, the gray, and Father Estevan to fend for themselves.

Lawrence? he wondered. Or Wilhelm? It could be both of them. It was unlikely, though, that there would be a gang of Mexican toughs backing up Lawrence tonight. Not since their pay would have to come out of Lawrence's own pocket now that he'd been fired.

Matt stopped dead still once he got out of the open roadway and into the brush. In here his ears were of far greater importance than his eyes.

He stood in silence, listening, waiting for the shooter to make a mistake.

Matt did not have long to wait. Matt had come off the paint so quickly that the ambusher must have thought he'd hit his target and that Matt was down.

Apparently anxious to finish the job, the gunman broke cover and came out of hiding almost immediately. The man was not very good in the woods. He made as much noise as a bull elk in rut.

Matt palmed his Colt and moved toward the approaching sounds. He positioned himself slightly to one side of the fellow's route and stepped inside the spread of branches on a stunted cedar, letting the foliage, such as it was, break his outline and help to conceal him from view.

The crackle and pop of incautious movement came nearer, and a dark figure soon appeared heading toward a patch of open ground immediately in front of Matt. The ambusher was indeed Lawrence, as Matt could easily see by the shape of his hat creases and the set of his shoulders.

He was carrying a rifle held at waist level.

Matt waited until Lawrence was a pace beyond the cedar, then spoke.

"Drop it!"

Lawrence would not have jumped any harder or any higher if Matt had rammed the sharp end of a bayonet into his kidneys. "Wha . . ."

"Drop it," Matt warned again.

It was excellent advice, but Lawrence did not take it. Instead he himself dropped to one knee, swiveling around as he did so.

He tried to lift the Winchester to his shoulder.

Matt could not afford to take silly chances with an armed man who was intent on murder. Matt's Colt roared, and a sheet of yellow flame obscured Lawrence from view and momentarily blurred Matt's vision.

Matt heard a hollow sound like a muted cough, a clatter, which he knew was the rifle falling onto hard soil, and then a softer, more muted thump, which he took to be the sound of Lawrence hitting the ground.

Taking no chances, Matt moved quickly, if blindly, to the side, but there was no return gunfire.

Matt shook his head and blinked rapidly trying to restore

his vision. When he could see again, he saw that Lawrence was down and would stay that way. Blood pooled black and shiny in the faint starlight from above, and the man's chest showed no hint of movement.

Loud crashing and crackling came from the direction of the road, and Matt whirled, Colt ready, but it was Father Estevan who burst into view.

The priest asked something in Spanish. Matt did not know the words, but he was sure of their meaning anyway. He pointed toward Lawrence lying still warm in sudden death.

Father Estevan dropped to his knees beside the body.

"I'll go get your stuff, Father, so you can say whatever it is that's gotta be said over him. Then we can carry him with us an' bury him tomorrow the same time as we put Pete in the ground."

It did not seem to matter a whit that neither Matt nor Father Estevan understood each other. Each knew what had to be done.

Matt fetched the padre's gear from the gray and gave the bundle to Father Estevan, then slipped back into the brush. He wanted to find Lawrence's horse—it had to be somewhere fairly nearby—so they could carry the body on with them to the Branvol place.

CHAPTER 38

The brothers were hot, sweaty, and near worn out from digging in the clay-heavy, gravel-laden soil on the bench above the Branvol house, but unpleasant though it was, it was a job that had to be done. Both of them retreated to the shade while Father Estevan, Anita, and a weeping little boy said what had to be said and did what had to be done for the man named Lawrence—none of them knew his last name—and for Peter Constantine Branvol.

Father Estevan concluded the solemn service, closed the Bible in his hands, and made the sign of the cross above each grave. Then Anita and the boy Ricardo each picked up a handful of gravel to toss onto Pete's body. There was no coffin and no wood to build one, so he was laid to rest still wrapped inside Matt's bedroll tarp. Lawrence did not have that much; they simply laid him in the bottom of the grave and put a kerchief over his face to keep the dirt off. It was done as a matter of respect for humankind, and not out of any regard for this particular very flawed example of the breed.

When Anita and the boy took Father Estevan inside, Sam and Matt picked up their shovels again and moved forward to fill the graves. They would fashion crosses to set at the heads of the graves later.

"You pleased me last night, you know," Sam observed when they paused to take a breather before a final assault on the task.

"How's that?"

"When you told me that Wilhelm is still alive. He must not have been there when Koronado and his men struck. I am glad. When we run into him again, Matt, he is mine. I owe him."

"I don't have any quarrel with that, brother. After what he did t' you when you couldn't fight back, yeah, I figure you do owe him."

"It is a debt I will repay with interest compounded."

"Fair enough, Sam, fair enough."

They filled both graves and mounded them, then searched along the bench for flat slabs of shale to use as makeshift paving that would serve to discourage animals from digging into them. Nothing could keep out the small burrowing animals, but they did what they reasonably could.

They were almost finished when Father Estevan and Anita came outside. The priest got his horse and climbed rather awkwardly onto it. Anita and he spoke briefly; then the padre reined away and started off toward town. Anita watched him for a moment, then walked up to where Matt and Sam were working.

"Should one of us ride with him to see that he gets back all right?" Matt asked.

Anita shook her head. "He travels with the hand of God protecting him. He will be fine," she said. "He asked me to give you his thanks, both of you. He said he will pray for your souls."

"What can we do for you?" Sam asked. "Are you and the boy all right?"

"Things will never be the same. Never. But we will survive. I have asked the good father to send a message to my family. Our farm is poor, but their hearts are good and their hands willing. They will come here. Together we will work this land. The cattle. Maybe farm a little. Together we will go on."

"I'm glad," Matt told her. "I know Pete would be pleased to know that you're gonna be all right."

"Yes, this is true. He would be. May I ask you something?"

"Of course," Sam said. "Anything."

Matt nodded his agreement with that sentiment.

"You did not say what it was that happened to my wonderful Peter. Where was it that you found him exactly?"

It was Sam who answered. He turned and pointed up the mountain. "There. High up. There is an old Spanish mine. We found him on a slope of loose rock just below the old arrastra."

Anita looked puzzled. "Whatever could Peter have been doing up there? That old thing is useless, just like the ground around it. We cannot get the cattle up that high for summer grazing. It is too steep to go directly up and too far around otherwise. The don we bought this place from did not even charge us for those hectares when we calculated the price."

Sam and Matt exchanged startled looks. It was Matt who blurted out the question both of them were thinking. "*You* own that ground?"

Anita attached no particular importance to the question. "Yes, of course. But as I say, it is useless to us. We have no way to go there except too far around to be worth the trouble. But we went there to see it when we first looked at this land.

"Neither Peter nor I knew anything about mines, but we looked. We even took pieces of rock from there and carried them to San Iba. We showed them to Lieutenant Espinosa, but he does not know anything about such things either. He was kind enough to take the rocks from us and send them to a friend who is knowledgeable about these things. They are worthless. We already were quite sure of that, but it was good of the *alcalde* to confirm that this was so."

"Yes," Matt mused. "Mighty good of him."

"Isn't it just," Sam concurred.

Anita lifted her face toward the sky, her expression wistful. "It was a good day that day we rode up to the mine. We went all of us together." She managed a laugh. "Poor little Ricardo had no choice about this for he was not yet born. But he was with us just the same."

Then the young widow's expression crumbled and the tears began to flow, prompted by memories of a far happier time.

She stamped her foot in anger at her own outburst, then gathered up her skirts and ran for the sanctuary of the home she had shared with her beloved Pete.

"I'll be dang," Matt said.

"Yes, exactly. No wonder Williams and Espinosa were ragging Pete. They were stealing from him and Anita. Whatever it is they're taking out of the ground up there, all of it belongs to Anita."

"Explains why they killed him too. Once he found out just where it was they were mining, on his own land but without his permission, they either had to pay up or get him out of the way."

"A bullet is cheaper than a going mine."

"Kinda cold, those gents," Matt said.

"Tell me, Matt," Sam said, his lips thinning into a cold, deadly smile, "do you think we should discuss this with them?"

"Yeah. Yeah, brother, I kinda think that we should."

"We'll stay here today and see what we can do to help Anita and the boy get settled a little. Then tomorrow, why don't we take a little ride into San Iba."

Matt nodded, his expression grim. "Yeah. Let's."

CHAPTER 39

It was late morning by the time the brothers reached San Iba. The town was quiet and pleasant, with ladies both American and Mexican visiting on the sidewalks and children playing in the vacant lots and alleys . . . and in the streets whenever their mothers did not notice.

A few horsemen were visible, and there were wagons and buggies parked along the rails in the business district. Stray dogs and wandering chickens crossed the road.

Sam and Matt rode the length of the street to Doc Tippett's place and dismounted to lead their horses inside, Sam on his own good mount and Matt with the rented paint.

"Come to get your horse back, have you?" Doc asked.

"Ayuh, I have," Matt told him.

"He could use more rest than this. You used him hard before you brought him in here."

"Yes, sir, I know, but I need him."

The hostler frowned. "Fine. He's your horse." It was obvious that Doc disapproved of putting the bay back under saddle without another day or more of rest and good feed.

"We have some traveling to do, my brother and me. Slow, though. I won't be asking more'n a road jog out of him."

Doc grumbled but finally, grudgingly, assented. "That won't hurt him. Prob'ly."

"We'll leave Sam's horse and all our gear here for a little while if that's all right with you, Doc. We have to do some shopping. Lay in some supplies. We'll come back soon as we're done over at the mercantile. We'd appreciate it if you'd figure up what we owe you. We can settle up before we leave."

"You aren't coming back?" Tippett seemed mildly surprised. "I thought you came here to visit with your friend."

"We could be back, but we don't know that for sure. Anyway, Pete is dead."

"Dead! How? What happened?"

Sam answered before Matt might blurt out the truth or something too close to it for Anita's comfort. "We found him under a slide of rock and shale up on the mountain above his place."

"That's terrible."

"Yes, indeed it is."

Tippett had no idea just how terrible it was, murder being a terrible thing indeed, but they had no intention of telling Doc or anyone else about that aspect of Pete's death. Yet.

The plan the brothers had come up with before they set out from the ranch that morning was that Anita and Ricardo would say nothing. She and the boy would wait there for her family to join her. Matt and Sam would ride to a town called Rancho Diego, which was the military headquarters for this district of northern Mexico.

They had neither the intention of nor the desire to start a war with the entire Mexican Army. After all, with odds of several thousand to one against them, even the blood brothers did not feel confident of victory. In this case, they agreed, discretion would be in order. They would ride to Rancho Diego and have a word with the district commander in the hope that he could offer some measure of justice to the young widow from San Iba.

Maybe he could offer a prison cell or better yet a hangman's rope to Lieutenant Antonio Espinosa too, they hoped.

Now all they needed was food enough to carry them for a few days until they reached Rancho Diego. Wherever that was.

"Say, Doc."

"Mmm?" Tippett finished cleaning out the paint's hoof and set the foot down, straightening his own back with a grimace. "I swear I'd give this business up and retire to a nice little place over on the coast if I could find anybody fool enough to buy it. Do you boys want a livery stable? Cheap. No? Oh, well. Now, what's your question, Matt?"

"D'you know a place called Rancho Diego?"

"Of course. It's an actual ranch, by the way, not a town. Belongs to the governor of this district. I hear he's got himself an Army garrison and Lord knows what-all else there. What do you need the governor for?"

Sam and Matt exchanged glances. A governor was likely even better for their purposes than a military commander. A civil officer was more likely to want to help one of his citizens than an Army officer. Their plan shifted in that direction without either one of them having to utter a word about it.

They would appeal to the governor on behalf of Anita and her family. Hopefully he would take care of Antonio Espinosa. The brothers, however, wanted to handle

Jarold Williams themselves. They intended to do that as soon as they returned from Rancho Diego.

"We heard there is a man at this Rancho Diego place that we want to talk with but we don't know where it is," Sam said.

"It's easy enough found," Tippett said. "Will you be gone long?"

"I don't know," Matt told him. "How long will it take to go there and come back again?"

Doc smiled. "I didn't mean it that way. You said you want to go buy some things for the traveling. Will you be at the store very long?"

"Oh. Not very, I suppose. You know. We'll just pick up a little of this, little of that."

"Give me twenty minutes or a half hour. I'll get your horse ready, Matt, and make you up a sack of grain to carry with you. And I'll draw you out a map of how to get from here to Rancho Diego without going all the way back up to the border. I can save you a half day of travel."

"Thanks, Doc. We appreciate it."

"A half hour then."

"You've got it. Thanks."

The brothers walked out into the bright sunshine on San Iba's main street.

"I dunno, Sam. D'you think we should go over to the hotel and have some lunch before we set out?"

"No," Sam told him. "The last time I set foot in that place I got thrown in prison for being an uppity Indian. I think what we need to do is buy what we need and stay out of sight until Doc has the horses and that sketch ready."

"All right. We'll go straight over to the mercantile and make our purchases, then go around back to the alley and find a shady spot where we can open some cans and make a quick lunch that way."

"That sounds better, Matt." Sam looked around at the quiet, pleasant street. "There is something about this town that I do not like, brother."

"Your imagination acting up on you again, is it?"

"Call it imagination if you like, but you know I have been right more times than you probably care to admit."

Matt nodded. "Yeah. Reckon you have. So this time I'll go along with you. We'll walk straight over to the store, get what we gotta get, and then leave. We can hunker down and have a bite to eat out back of Doc's corrals. How does that sound?"

"Reasonable," Sam said. "I like the sound of it."

"Consider it done then."

The brothers strode swiftly down the sidewalk, their boot heels thumping on the boards and their spurs chiming merrily.

CHAPTER 40

"I'd like ten cents worth o' those licorice sticks, please."

Sam grinned. "Sweet tooth bothering you, brother?"

"Yeah, it is. Prob'ly the same one that made you buy that poke of horehound candies."

The grin turned into a wince. "I thought I'd gotten away with that."

"Nothing escapes ol' Eagle Eye here," Matt said.

"That's your Indian name, is it?"

"If it isn't, then it oughta be. Thank you," Matt said to the young woman behind the counter when she handed him his licorice. Then he tilted his head and gave her a speculative look. The proprietor's daughter, he supposed. She was not bad. Blond, pale, brown-eyed, twenty or thereabouts. A trifle on the skinny side. But not bad. It seemed a pity they had to leave so soon.

"Is that everything?" Sam asked. He began rummaging through the burlap sack of foods they had purchased. "Hmm. Tinned meat. Jerky. Flour. Honey. Hardtack. Canned peaches. Coffee."

"Already ground, I hope."

"Yes, Matt, it's already been ground."

"Salt. Did you get salt?"

"We have salt."

"And bacon."

"I didn't get any bacon."

"Miss, would you please add some bacon? Half a side of it."

"Half a side!" Sam protested. "It will get everything around it greasy."

"Would you please wrap the bacon real good, miss," Matt said. To Sam he added, "I'll carry the bacon separate if you like."

"Darn right I do. I don't want all that salt and grease getting in my saddlebags."

"I said I'd carry it, didn't I?"

"Fine. See that you do."

"Will that be all?" the blond girl asked.

"I think so. Is there anything else you want, Matt?"

"No, this should do."

The girl added up a column of figures she'd been jotting down on the roll of brown wrapping paper beside the counter and said, "That will be four dollars and sixty-two cents."

"Pay the lady, brother," Sam said. He picked up the bulkier of the two sacks of groceries they had selected, leaving Matt with the heavier sack containing the bacon. And the licorice.

Matt handed over a five-dollar half eagle in U.S. money and collected his change, a mixture of Mexican and American coins. He was not sure if the change was correct, but decided to assume that it was rather than try to convert the Mexican coins to some measure that he understood. Besides, the little lady looked like she could be trusted.

"Thank you, miss." Matt touched the brim of his Stetson and followed Sam to the back of the store, where a door looked like it should lead into the alley behind the block of buildings.

Just as Matt reached the doorway, Sam came bursting

backward into him, nearly knocking him off his feet. "Hey, watch it!" Matt said.

"Hush."

"What?"

"I said hush, Matt. I think . . . wait a minute." Sam removed his own wide-brimmed Stetson and leaned against the doorjamb, pulling the door open a fraction of an inch and peering out.

"Trouble?"

"Uh-huh," Sam said. "Big trouble. There are two men out there. I recognize them from the mine. They work as guards there. They work for Jarold Williams."

"D'you think someone saw us on the street and recognized us?"

Sam shrugged. "Your guess is as good as mine, but I'd say that pretty much has to be what happened."

"I'll check out front. Maybe we can go out that way." He returned a few moments later. "Your pal Wilhelm is hiding behind a barrel on the left, and there are a couple men with guns standing close beside the building to the right."

"If Wilhelm is hiding how did you. . . ."

"I didn't say he was doing a very good job of it," Matt put in before Sam could finish.

"Come to throw a party for us, have they?"

"Yeah, and you know what kinda party it would be. The same kind they gave to Pete would be my guess. They're serious, Sam, and they got shotguns. It's awful hard to outrun a load of buckshot, and even a lousy shot can hit a target big as a man."

"What do you suggest we do now?"

Matt looked around the store with its shelves and boxes and bundles of goods. "Well, we aren't gonna run out of food or ammunition. So I'd think we should send the young lady an' her family out of the line o' fire, then see can we whittle the odds down before we even think about making a break for it."

"A siege, you mean."

"Yeah, Sam, I guess that I do. It's either that or surrender to them, an' somehow I don't think that would be a very good idea."

"Unfortunately, I agree," Sam said. "In that case. . . ." He closed and bolted the back door, then took up a position at the front. "You're the charmer, Matt. I'll leave it up to you to get the lady and her family out."

Somewhere in the street outside a shotgun boomed, the muzzle report flat and dull, and immediately afterward one of the front windows of the mercantile exploded inward in a shower of glass.

The blond girl screamed and ran out the back door.

Matt closed and rebolted the door behind her. "Reckon I took care of that in jig time."

Sam crouched near the broken front window surveying the street beyond. After a moment he lifted his Colt, took careful aim, and squeezed off a shot.

There was a fusillade of answering fire, but no damage was done.

"First blood to our side," Sam said calmly.

"You dropped one?"

Sam grinned. "No, but that one will have a miserable time trying to sit down for the next few weeks or so."

Shotguns and revolvers roared along the street for a few moments, and then fell silent again.

"There are more of them than I thought," Sam said. "This could be a long afternoon."

"I don't mind," Matt said. "Just as long as we're both here to see the end of it." He tipped a flour barrel on its side and rolled it toward the front windows to begin building a barricade.

CHAPTER 41

"Matt, we have to break out of here."

"Now there's an original thought." Matt raised his revolver, sighted carefully down the barrel, and nicked the heel of someone's very slightly exposed boot. Across the street the man howled, more in surprise than pain, and drew his leg in. Matt flipped open the loading gate on his Colt, shucked the empty cartridge casing, and dropped in a fat brass round to replace it. That was one nice thing. They had the entire store stock of shells to fire if need be; they were not likely to run out of ammunition.

"It will be dark soon. I think we should make a break out the back. Is that man still there?"

"I'll look," said Matt. Of the original two who had been in the alley, one had disappeared sometime during the afternoon and had not come back.

Matt crossed the store to the back door, but instead of giving himself away by opening it, climbed onto the stepladder they'd placed there earlier. He removed his hat and peered out through the transom. The glass panel in the transom had been painted over, but enough of the paint had flaked away that in some places it was possible to see through.

"The man is still there," Matt reported once he returned to the windows at the front, both of which were broken now and lying in pieces across the floor. "I'm not sure what he's doing. Picking a scab or something. Anyway, he isn't paying much attention to the door."

"And he doesn't have his gun in his hands?"

Matt shook his head.

"Then why don't we slip out and have a word with him?"

"We?" Matt said.

"You know good and well that I am better at this sort of thing than you are."

"I don't know any such thing."

"I do. But have it your way. We can flip a coin for it."

"That sounds fair."

"Let me take a look first. I want to see what we will be up against. I'll be right back."

Matt kept an eye on the street where Williams and his men were concentrated. A few moments later he felt a flow of fresh air on the back of his neck. When he turned to see where it was coming from, he saw that the ladder had been moved and the back door was standing slightly ajar. There was no sign of Sam August Webster Two-Wolves.

"Dang you, Sam," he whispered.

Sam was gone only a minute or two. When he came back, he stepped inside and crossed the store in a crouch. "Give me two or three minutes, then throw a couple shots out the window. Come down through the alley to the livery. I will have the horses ready."

"What'd you do with the guard?"

Sam grinned. "He's enjoying a nice nap. But I predict he may have a headache when he wakes up." Sam picked up the bags of supplies they'd purchased earlier and laid another coin on the counter to cover anything they had consumed during the afternoon, either by eating it, drinking it, or shooting it. "Three minutes," he whispered, then he was gone.

Matt threw a random shot out the window, fired again, and then reloaded. Out in the street there was a flurry of answering gunfire.

It was almost fully dark by the time Matt slipped inside the livery barn, Colt in hand just in case something had gone wrong.

"It's all right, Matt." The voice was not Sam's, though, and Matt very nearly shot the half-seen figure who spoke to him.

"Doc. Is that you? Where's Sam?"

"In back saddling the horses. I told him I would keep watch here so I could shout a warning if Williams or one of his people came."

"Thanks."

"It is good you boys made your break while you still could. Lieutenant Espinosa is up on the mountain trying to round up all his men and bring them down here. He sent them to find the runaway slaves and bring them back. Now he wants them to lay siege to the mercantile." Tippett shook his head. "I'm glad he isn't here for more than one reason. That fool Espinosa would probably try to burn you out and set the whole town on fire."

Sam came into the barn from the back. "I have the horses ready."

"Do you intend for us to make a run for it or try an' sneak out quiet?" Matt asked.

"Sneak," Sam said. "I wrapped the horses' feet in burlap to soften their sound. We can remove the wrapping when we are clear."

"All right." Matt turned to Tippett. "Doc, thanks. You've been a real friend."

"Truth is, I've enjoyed meeting you boys. I wish we had more of your kind around here and less"—he inclined his head in the direction of the mercantile where there was still a little desultory shooting doing on in the street, Williams and his men not yet having figured out that the rabbits had bolted—"less of their sort. Good luck."

Sam and Matt went out into what was now full darkness. The moon was not yet up, and the only light in the sky was from the stars.

"Doc acts like he thinks we won't be back," Matt said as he swung into his saddle.

"Doc does not know us very well, does he," Sam answered.

The brothers reined their horses away from the sounds of gunfire and headed very quietly out of San Iba.

CHAPTER 42

"Feels a little different riding in this way, doesn't it," Matt observed five days later when the blood brothers returned to San Iba.

The big difference lay in the fact that this time they were entering the town at the head of a troop of Mexican cavalry commanded by Major Oswaldo de la Rosa.

"We'll drop out here an' see to our horses," Matt told the officer when they reached the edge of town. "We'll join you as soon as they're settled."

"Very well, gentlemen. My men will set up camp. Then we shall see what we shall see, eh?"

"So we shall," Sam said. "So we shall."

The brothers dismounted at the doors to the livery, and watched the seventy or so gaudily uniformed troopers pass by in a column of twos, guidon and national flag snapping in a stiff breeze. A trio of dogs came rushing out to get underfoot, and almost everyone in the community came out onto the sidewalks to watch this procession.

"Considering the way you left out of here, I didn't expect to see you boys again," Doc Tippett said as he came outside wiping his hands on a greasy rag, his legs covered by an equally filthy blacksmith's leather apron.

"How'd you manage all this? Surely the governor didn't take your word about conditions here."

"No, but then we didn't ask him to," Matt responded. "We gave him our side of it, of course, but we suggested—"

"*Who* suggested?" Sam interrupted.

"Okay, *Sam* suggested that the governor send someone honorable an' trustworthy to look things over and talk with Espinosa first, then also with a number of townspeople, before he makes up his mind about how things are here. It will be up to the major out there what if anything oughta be done after that."

"Well, the man will certainly get an earful from me," Tippett said.

"We suggested that you be on the list of people he should talk to, Doc. You and Father Estevan and the other leaders in the community, Mexican and Anglo alike. Governor Hernandez sent his best man. He said we can trust the major to be scrupulously fair."

"If he does that," Doc said, "and if he's as fair as he is claimed to be, lads, then I think our *alcalde* will be finding himself out of a job and this place will be the better for it."

"Too late to do any good for our friend Pete, though," Matt lamented.

"I heard what happened to him, boys. Anita came in to buy supplies and to go to Mass. She was still upset. She told everyone she saw that day, and Father Estevan confirmed the things she said. It's all around town by now. The whole community knows, and they have come down hard against Jarold Williams and Espinosa. Folks were already pretty unhappy about Williams and his bunch shooting up the place when they thought they had you cornered that day. That already set the mood, and Anita Branvol's story was the icing on the cake. The lieutenant has been staying out of sight for the past couple days. I have no idea where Williams has gotten to."

Sam looked at Matt, and received a nod from his brother without a word passing between them.

"Doc, we've changed our minds about putting our horses up right now. There's something we need t' do first. Would you please explain to Major de la Rosa that we'll be back quick as we can?"

"Sure, whatever you say."

Sam handed Matt the reins to his horse. "Excuse me for a moment, brother."

Even Matt was uncertain what Sam was up when he disappeared inside the livery. He came back outside moments later.

Sam had dipped two fingers into the pot of axle grease Tippett had been using in there, and smeared the black grease in ragged swipes across his forehead and onto each cheek.

It might not be exactly traditional, but there was no reason the grease could not serve more than adequately as war paint.

By unspoken consent, the brothers drew rein a quarter mile short of the gate leading into the mine. They dismounted and tied the horses out of sight from the road.

"Let me observe from above," Sam said. "I will signal down to you if I see anything."

"All right. I'll be ready."

Sam quickly scaled a cut-bank above the road and disappeared into the sparse brush. Matt checked his rifle and then his Colt before giving his Stetson a tug and setting out cautiously along the side of the road. Jarold Williams and his crew—whatever was left of it—would very likely have a sentinel posted.

A hundred yards down the road, Matt paused and chuckled softly to himself. A Winchester rifle lay in the middle of the road, its stock broken at the grip.

Above that spot he could see an unconscious man slumped against the bole of a slender pine. It took Matt a moment to realize that the guard's hands appeared to be tied behind him and around the tree. Sam had already been busy up there.

Matt walked more swiftly after that. He did not want to get too far behind and miss out on all the fun.

As quickly as he moved, though, Sam was still ahead of him. When Matt reached the mine buildings and again slowed his pace, Sam stepped out of the blacksmith's shop and stood in plain sight to motion Matt forward.

"They're all inside," Sam said, hooking a thumb over his shoulder at the old mine headquarters building that had more recently served as a bunkhouse for the guards.

"Is Williams with them?" Matt asked.

"That I do not know." A glint that might have been mistaken for mirth—but was not—appeared in his dark eyes. "Case Wilhelm is there, though. I heard his voice clearly."

"Your pal," Matt said.

"Yes. Isn't he."

"How d'you want to do this?"

Sam's dark face, its broad planes highlighted by the black war paint, creased into something resembling a smile. "Wait here. I will . . . shall we say . . . ask them to come outside."

Matt nodded, then asked, "Any idea how many of 'em are in there?"

"No. Do you care?"

"Nope. Just curious."

"Give me a few minutes and you can count them."

Sam first went into the nearby tool shed and emerged carrying a bundle of dirty, much-used cloth, several of the canvas sacks that were used to haul minerals up from the arrastra to be packed and shipped away for refining.

Draping the canvas over his shoulder, Sam went to the rear of the bunkhouse and scaled the corner, using the notches in the logs like rungs on a ladder to reach the roof. Once there, he moved very carefully toward the chimney at the roof peak, his moccasins making no sound on the dry timbers the way boot heels would have.

Sam reached inside his shirt and pulled out several handfuls of green moss that he must have gathered in the woods after they left the horses. His expression set in a grim satisfied smile, he first dropped the moss inside the chimney to create smoke as soon as it hit whatever coals were below, then draped the thick canvas over the chimney opening.

After that Sam stood waiting on the roof while Matt remained where he was at ground level.

Their wait was not a long one.

Three burly men came outside, then Case Wilhelm, and finally one more guard. Five men in all. None of them was armed. But then they came out not for a fight, but to escape the thick smoke that was billowing out through the newly opened door, and even seeping from under the eaves of the roof where Sam stood watching. They came out stumbling and cursing and rubbing their eyes.

Three of the men were barefoot and only partially dressed, but Wilhelm held onto his precious bamboo flail, precious, that is, to him. He carried it as if it were a badge of high office.

Matt opened his mouth to ask if these four were all who had been inside, but the question was answered before it was uttered by the sound of coughing from inside the old building. Matt moved over closer to the front wall so he could not be seen from inside. If the person who remained in there wanted trouble, Matt did not want to make it easy for him by offering himself as a target.

Wilhelm raised his chin and loudly called, "You can

come on out, Mr. Williams. It's that fella I told you about that called hisself Tam O'Shanter." Matt guessed that Wilhelm had not yet seen Sam up there on the roof.

Louder still, Wilhelm hollered, "He knows you're in there, Mr. Williams. He heard you coughing. He's to the left of the door. Be careful. He has a rifle."

Matt was only mildly annoyed with Wilhelm for giving such a complete warning. After all, Jarold Williams was Wihelm's employer and a man rightly should show loyalty to his own.

A moment later Williams coughed some more and called, "Don't shoot. I'm coming out."

He stepped into view in the doorway and stood there rubbing the stinging smoke from his eyes while tears streamed down his cheeks. He blinked and sucked in clean, smoke-free air for a moment, then looked around to find Matt standing nearby.

"You. You and that friend of yours have ruined everything," Williams said accusingly.

"That man is my friend," Matt agreed. "He's also my brother. You and your friends came near to killing him. Would've killed him if you'd had your way about it. An' you did kill a friend of mine. Pete Branvol was a better man than you'll ever know, mister, yet you and that fancy lieutenant killed him and a whole lot of other folks. It's time you two are called to account for your sins."

"You have killed men," Williams said.

"Yes, I have," Matt agreed, "and every one of them had his fair chance at me an' each one for a reason. What about you, mister? You have a hogleg on your hip. Do you want to try me?"

"No. I am not a gunfighter. I've seen you shoot. I know how fast you are. Here. Wait." Williams carefully unfastened his gun belt, and let it slide down his leg to thump solidly onto the ground. "There. I'm not armed now."

The man stepped a few paces closer to Matt, and

stood with his legs slightly spread and his hands clasped at his waist.

There was something about the tension in the set of the man's shoulders and a tightness in his jaw that told Matt things might not be all they appeared.

Matt took half a step backward and let his right hand fall free and relaxed to his side.

Jarold Williams squeezed his forearms hard against his belly and spring-loaded gambler rigs hidden inside his sleeves snapped a pair of dark, deadly little derringers into his waiting hands.

A crooked smile began to form on the man's lips.

And then froze there.

Matt Bodine's Colt was already in his hand. And there was already a sheet of flame blossoming from the muzzle of his revolver.

A .44-caliber bullet impacted Jarold Williams's breastbone and rocked him back on his heels.

A second slug struck the side of his chest and turned him halfway around.

Williams found it difficult to draw breath. His chest was shattered and his lungs torn. His vision was clouding. He blinked but could see . . . nothing. He could hear his own labored gasps as he fought for breath, and the crunch of gravel under boot leather.

There was a ringing in his ears and a sound like rushing water.

Then a veil descended onto him and he could no longer hear or see anything at all.

"Dead," someone said very distantly.

And then there was nothing.

CHAPTER 43

"He was supposed to be a fast man with a gun," one of the guards blurted out as they stood over Jarold Williams's lifeless body.

"It's a funny thing about that," Matt observed aloud, Colt still in his hand. "Something every man who's fast with a gun oughta know and every fellow who isn't fast does know. That is that somewhere out there there's sure t' be someone who's faster."

"Even faster than you, mister?"

Matt grinned, then tipped his head back and laughed. "That rule applies to everybody except me, o' course."

Smoke continued to pour out of the old headquarters building, and when Sam climbed down from the roof he looked like an avenging angel—or devil—traversing the walkways of Hades.

"You!" Case Wilhelm blurted out. "Are you behind all this?"

"No, you are. You and that man lying dead there and the Mexican popinjay who by now should be under arrest in town. You are the ones who brought it down upon yourselves. My brother and I are only the instruments of destruction. You yourselves are the cause."

Wilhelm sneered. "Fact remains, you cowered at my feet."

"Fact remains, I was in chains then. Now I am not." Sam nodded to the others and said, "You four move over there where my brother can keep an eye on you. Wilhelm, you can stand right where you are. Or you can drop to your knees and beg. Whichever you prefer."

"Get down on my knees for a stinking Injun? That will be the day."

"That's right. This will indeed be the day." Sam unbuckled his gun belt and draped it over a corner notch on the log mine building. He stripped off his shirt and hung it over the holstered Colt and perched his hat on top of that.

"What's this, Injun? Do you think you can best me?" Wilhelm said, contempt thick in his tone of voice.

"Yes," was Sam's simple answer. "I do."

Wilhelm's hand flashed and the bamboo flail sang nastily as it whipped through the air. A good eight feet separated Wilhelm from Sam, so Wilhelm's intent obviously was to intimidate.

Sam Two-Wolves did not act like he was much intimidated.

And this time there were no chains to bind him.

Wilhelm's flail sang again, but this time Sam stepped in behind it, moving with deceptive speed.

Wilhelm lifted the flail. Sam ignored it. He moved in close and delivered a sharp left to Wilhelm's short ribs. That drove the wind out of the bigger man and brought his hand reflexively down.

Before Wilhelm realized what he was up to, Sam snatched the bamboo flail away from him and then quickly faded backward. This time Sam Two-Wolves was the one who held the flail.

Smiling coldly, Sam raised the flail. Wilhelm lifted his elbows to protect his eyes from the expected cut of the bamboo. Instead Sam took the flail in both hands and snapped it in two.

Contemptuously, he tossed the shattered and now useless scraps of bamboo onto the ground at Wilhelm's feet.

The big man stared in disbelief, looking as if it were he and not merely some strips of bamboo that had been broken.

"You . . . you oughtn't to've . . . to've done that."

Sam said nothing. He stepped in close and flicked another hard left, this time his punch landing on the bridge of Wilhelm's nose. Cartilage snapped and blood sprayed from the freshly broken nose. Wilhelm rocked back on his heels.

Sam drilled him with a series of repeated lefts to the face, then a devastating right to the breadbasket that doubled the big man over and dropped him to his knees. Sam stepped back. And waited.

But there was no fight in Wilhelm now. When he looked up, there were tears streaming down his face and snot mixed in with the blood that ran from his nose.

"Gone," he mumbled. "Every . . . everything. All gone. All gone." There was a deep sadness in his voice.

Sam snorted contemptuously. "Get up, you coward. Get up and start thinking about what your life in a Mexican prison will be like."

Wilhelm seemed puzzled. "Prison?"

"Murder, Wilhelm. How many men have you murdered here? How many will they find when they dig that slope down the hill? Jarold Williams may have escaped the scales of justice, but you and your lieutenant friend won't. We are taking you to San Iba and then on to the governor's palace. You will stand trial, Wilhelm. If you are very, very lucky the governor will allow you to go to the gallows. If not . . . have you ever seen what the inside of a Mexican prison is like? I don't mean some little jail. I mean one of those stone-walled dungeons they call a prison down here. If I were you, Wilhelm, I would pray for that hangman's noose."

Wilhelm shook his head. He stared mutely for long moments at the shattered scraps that were all that remained of his flail . . . and of the authority he had wielded over other men here at this place.

Then with an anguished groan he came to his feet in a rush.

Sam prepared to defend himself, but Wilhelm's charge brushed past Sam.

Instead he lunged for the Colt that was hanging at the corner of the building.

Wilhelm's hand closed over the grip. He snatched the revolver free of leather and whirled.

A red dot appeared in the center of Wilhelm's forehead, the spot wet and lightly pulsing. Droplets of moisture shined ruby red in the sunlight behind him.

The big man's head snapped back and he dropped to his knees, Sam's Colt falling from suddenly lifeless fingers. Wilhelm pitched face-forward onto the hard ground. Stringy gobbets of gray and red brain matter dripped down the side of the building behind where Wilhelm had just been.

"Jeez," one of the guards blurted out. The man spun around and dropped to his knees to heave out whatever his last meal had been.

"Sorry to butt in," Matt apologized as he dropped his Colt back into its holster.

"I will forgive you," Sam said solemnly. He stepped around Case Wilhelm's body and reached for his shirt and hat and gun belt.

"You boys," Matt ordered. "Any of you wants to try something, don't. Otherwise you can start walking."

"Where—"

"San Iba," Matt answered before the man was done

asking his question. "The Mexican authorities are waiting there to see you. Now *walk!*"

Matt finished tacking one last flattened tin can onto the sturdy grain bin and stood back to admire his handiwork. "There," he said. "That oughta keep the rats out." He let the heavy lid fall closed, but Sam spoke up.

"Don't be in such a hurry to think that you are finished. We still have to pour the grain back into it."

This particular bin was supposed to hold a mixture of corn, milo, and barley to be used for chicken scratch. Several other larger bins held oats for the horses and a little corn that was given to calves being fattened for the family table rather than sale at auction.

"The place is looking well, wouldn't you say?"

Sam glanced outside. "Just in time too, I think."

"What d'you mean?"

By way of an answer Sam inclined his head toward the road to San Iba. A motley procession of milk cows and runny-nosed children was coming down the road, led by a pair of ancient, high-wheeled *carretas* of the type it was said the old-time Comancheros favored. The huge carts were drawn by tall, rangy oxen with gutta-percha bulbs affixed to the tips of their impressively broad horns.

"Company?" Matt suggested.

"More like family would be my guess," Sam answered. "I would say that Anita's people have arrived." He smiled. "It looks to me like they have come prepared to stay."

"That's just as well. We can't hang around forever, and Lord knows she needs help running this place. Even with whatever money she can get from renting out the mine up there"—Matt tilted his head in the direction of the mountainside that hung above the ranch—"it'd be tough on her, a widow woman with two little kids to raise."

"Anita will be fine. She has family and she has an income. Before long she will find herself another husband. Count on it."

"Poor Pete," Matt said. "It was a bad end for a good man."

"It can be like that, brother. We never know when or how or even why, but soon or late we all come to the end of our trail."

"Ain't you the little ray of sunshine today."

"Just trying to be realistic, that's all."

"Personally, I could use a little less realism and a little more fun." Matt tossed his tack hammer onto a nearby shelf, and somewhat more carefully set a box of carpet tacks beside it. "I have a question for you, Sam."

"All right."

"Have you ever been to California?"

"Not lately," Sam said. "Not lately, I haven't."

"We're practically there."

Sam grinned. "It is only—what—five hundred miles or so?"

"Yeah, something like that. Close enough anyhow. You want to go see what it's like over there? They say the grass is belly-deep to a tall horse and the señoritas are beautiful."

"Or the señoritas look like horses," Sam suggested.

"Close enough," Matt said with another grin. "D'you want to take a look for yourself?"

"You know me, always concerned about bailing you out of the trouble you keep getting us into." Sam carefully laid aside the tools he had been using to flatten tin cans with for their rat-proofing project. "Let's go meet Anita's family," he said.

"And tell her we'll be riding on now," Matt added.

"Yes. That too," Sam agreed with a warm smile for this man who was his blood brother. "That too."

The brothers walked out into the sunshine together, each with his thoughts already on whatever road lay ahead.

AFTERWORD
Notes from the Old West

In the small town where I grew up, there were two movie theaters. The Pavilion was one of those old-timey movie show palaces, built in the heyday of Mary Pickford and Charlie Chaplin—the silent era of the 1920s. By the 1950s, when I was a kid, the Pavilion was a little worn around the edges, but it was still the premier theater in town. They played all those big Technicolor biblical Cecil B. DeMille epics and corny MGM musicals. In Cinemascope, of course.

On the other side of town was the Gem, a somewhat shabby and run-down grind house with sticky floors and torn seats. Admission was a quarter. The Gem booked low-budget "B" pictures (remember the Bowery Boys?), war movies, horror flicks, and Westerns. I liked the Westerns best. I could usually be found every Saturday at the Gem, along with my best friend, Newton Trout, watching Westerns from 10 A.M. until my father came looking for me around suppertime. (Sometimes Newton's dad was dispatched to come fetch us.) One time, my dad came to get me right in the middle of *Abilene Trail*, which featured the now-forgotten Whip Wilson. My father became so engrossed in the action he sat down and watched the rest of it with us. We didn't get home until after dark, and my mother's meat loaf was a pan of gray ashes by the time we did. Though my father and I were both in the doghouse the next day, this remains one of my fondest childhood memories. There was Wild Bill Elliot, and Gene Autry, and Roy Rogers, and Tim Holt, and, a little later, Rod Cameron and Audie Murphy. Of these newcomers, I never missed an Audie Murphy Western, because Audie was sort of an antihero. Sure, he stood for law and order and was an honest man, but sometimes he had to go around the law to uphold it. If he didn't play fair, it was only because he felt hamstrung by the laws of the land. Whatever it took to get the bad guys, Audie did it. There were no finer points of law, no splitting of legal hairs. It was instant justice, devoid of long-winded lawyers, bored or biased jurors, or black-robed, often corrupt judges.

Steal a man's horse and you were the guest of honor at a necktie party.

Molest a good woman and you got a bullet in the heart or a rope around the gullet. Or at the very least, got the crap beat out of you. Rob a bank and face a hail of bullets or the hangman's noose.

Saved a lot of time and money, did frontier justice.

That's all gone now, I'm sad to say. Now you hear, "Oh, but he had a bad childhood" or "His mother didn't give him enough love" or "The homecoming queen wouldn't give him a second look and he has an inferiority complex." Or "cultural rage," as the politically correct bright boys refer to it. How many times have you heard some self-important defense attorney moan, "The poor kids were only venting their hostilities toward an uncaring society?"

Mule fritters, I say. Nowadays, you can't even call a punk a punk anymore. But don't get me started.

It was, "Howdy, ma'am" time too. The good guys, antihero or not, were always respectful to the ladies. They might shoot a bad guy five seconds after tipping their hat to a woman, but the code of the West demanded you be respectful to a lady.

Lots of things have changed since the heyday of the Wild West, haven't they? Some for the good, some for the bad.

I didn't have any idea at the time that I would someday write about the West. I just knew that I was captivated by the Old West.

When I first got the itch to write, back in the early 1970s, I didn't write Westerns. I started by writing horror and action adventure novels. After more than two dozen novels, I began thinking about developing a Western character. From those initial musings came the novel *The Last Mountain Man: Smoke Jensen*. That was followed by *Preacher: The First Mountain Man*. A few years later, I began developing the Last Gunfighter series. Frank Morgan is a legend in his own time, the fastest gun west of the Mississippi . . . a title and a reputation he never wanted, but can't get rid of.

The Gunfighter series is set in the waning days of the Wild West. Frank Morgan is out of time and place, but still, he is pursued by men who want to earn a reputation as the man who killed the legendary gunfighter. All Frank wants to do is live in peace. But he knows in his heart that dream will always be just that: a dream, fog and smoke and mirrors, something elusive that will never really come to fruition. He will be forced to wander the West, alone, until one day his luck runs out.

For me, and for thousands—probably millions—of other people (although many will never publicly admit it), the old Wild West will always be a magic, mysterious place: a place we love to visit through the pages of books; characters we would like to know . . . from a safe distance; events we would love to take part in, again, from a safe distance. For the old Wild West was not a place for the faint of heart. It was a hard, tough, physically demanding time. There were no police to call if one faced adversity. One faced trouble alone, and handled it alone. It was rugged individualism: something that appeals to many of us.

I am certain that is something that appeals to most readers of Westerns.

I still do on-site research (whenever possible) before starting a Western novel. I have wandered over much of the West, prowling what is left of ghost towns. Stand in the midst of the ruins of these old towns, use a little bit of imagination, and one can conjure up life as it used to be in the Wild West. The rowdy Saturday nights, the tinkling of a piano in a saloon, the laughter of cowboys and miners letting off steam after a week of hard work. Use a little more imagination and one can envision two men standing in the street, facing one another, seconds before the hook and draw of a gunfight. A moment later, one is dead and the other rides away.

The old wild untamed West.

There are still some ghost towns to visit, but they are rapidly vanishing as time and the elements take their toll. If you want to see them, make plans to do so as soon as possible, for in a few years, they will all be gone.

And so will we.

Stand in what is left of the Big Thicket country of east Texas and try to imagine how in the world the pioneers managed to get through that wild tangle. I have wondered about that many times and marveled at the courage of the men and women who slowly pushed westward, facing dangers that we can only imagine.

Let me touch briefly on a subject that is very close to me: firearms. There are some so-called historians who are now claiming that firearms played only a very insignificant part in the settlers' lives. They claim that only a few were armed. What utter, stupid nonsense! What do these so-called historians think the pioneers did for food? Do they think the early settlers rode down to the nearest supermarket and bought their meat? Or maybe they think the settlers chased down deer or buffalo on foot and beat the animals to death with a club. I have a news flash for you so-called historians: The settlers used guns to shoot their game. They used guns to defend hearth and home against Indians on the warpath. They used guns to protect themselves from outlaws. Guns are a part of Americana. And always will be.

The mountains of the West and the remains of the ghost towns that dot those areas are some of my favorite subjects to write about. I have done extensive research on the various mountain ranges of the West and go back whenever time permits. I sometimes stand surrounded by the towering mountains and wonder how in the world the pioneers ever made it through. As hard as I try and as often as I try, I simply cannot imagine the hardships those men and women endured over the hard months of their incredible journey. None of us can. It is said that on the Oregon Trail alone, there are at least two bodies in lonely, unmarked graves for every mile of that journey. Some students of the West say the number of dead is at least twice that. And nobody knows the exact number of wagons that impatiently started out alone and simply vanished on the way, along with their occupants, never to be seen or heard from again.

Just vanished.

The one-hundred-and-fifty-year-old ruts of the wagon wheels can still be seen in various places along the Oregon Trail. But if you plan to visit those places, do so quickly, for they are slowly disappearing. And when they are gone, they will be lost forever, except in the words of Western writers.

As long as I can peck away at a keyboard and find a company to publish my work, I will not let the Old West die. That I promise you.

As The Drifter in the Last Gunfighter series, Frank Morgan has struck a responsive chord among the readers of frontier fiction. Perhaps it's because he is a human man, with all of the human frailties. He is not a superhero. He likes horses and dogs and treats them well. He has feelings and isn't afraid to show them or admit that he has them. He longs for a permanent home, a place to hang his hat and sit on the porch in the late afternoon and watch the day slowly fade into night . . . and a woman to share those simple pleasures with him. But Frank also knows he can never relax his vigil and probably will never have that long-wished-for hearth and home. That is why he is called The Drifter. Frank Morgan knows there are men who will risk their lives to face him in a hook and draw, slap leather, pull that big iron, in the hopes of killing the West's most famous gunfighter, so they can claim the title of the man who killed Frank Morgan, The Drifter. Frank would gladly, willingly, give them that title, but not at the expense of his own life.

So Frank Morgan must constantly drift, staying on the lonely trails, those out-of-the-way paths through the timber, the mountains, the deserts that are sometimes called the hoot-owl trail. His companions are the sighing winds, the howling of wolves, the yapping of coyotes, and a few, very few, precious memories. And his six-gun. Always, his six-gun.

Frank is also pursued by something else: progress. The towns are connected by telegraph wires. Frank is recognized wherever he goes and can be tracked by telegraphers. There is no escape for him. Reporters for various newspapers are always on his trail, wanting to interview Frank Morgan, as are authors, wanting to do more books about the legendary gunfighter. Photographers want to take his picture, if possible with the body of a man Frank has just killed. Frank is disgusted by the whole thing and wants no part of it. There is no real rest for The Drifter. Frank travels on, always on the move. He tries to stay off the more heavily traveled roads, sticking to lesser-known trails, sometimes making his own route of travel, across the mountains or deserts.

Someday perhaps Frank will find some peace. Maybe. But if he does, that is many books from now.

The West will live on as long as there are writers willing

to write about it, and publishers willing to publish it. Writing about the West is wide open, just like the old Wild West. Characters abound, as plentiful as the wide-open spaces, as colorful as a sunset on the Painted Desert, as restless as the ever-sighing winds. All one has to do is use a bit of imagination. Take a stroll through the cemetery at Tombstone, Arizona; read the inscriptions. Then walk the main street of that once-infamous town around midnight and you might catch a glimpse of the ghosts that still wander the town. They really do. Just ask anyone who lives there. But don't be afraid of the apparitions, they won't hurt you. They're just out for a quiet stroll.

The West lives on. And as long as I am alive, it always will.

Turn the page for an exciting preview of

BLOOD BOND:
SHOOTOUT AT GOLD CREEK

by William W. Johnstone

Coming in July 2006

Wherever Pinnacle Books are sold

CHAPTER 1

"We've got trouble, Boss."

Clarence Hart looked up from the machinery he was working on, his tanned skin glistening in the light of the setting sun. Touches of gray were sprinkled through his brown hair and laugh lines had started to form around his mouth. Though he was no longer a young man, years of hard work had made his muscles rock-hard and he was as strong as most men half his age. In this rough-and-tumble mining community composed almost exclusively of men, he worked shirtless. His shoulder muscles rippled as he stretched, trying to work out the kinks that laboring in a tight spot had given him.

The young man standing before him repeated his statement. "We've got trouble. It's Jordan's bunch. They're moving in on Shannahan down at the creek."

Hart clenched and unclenched his fists His blue eyes, usually twinkling with good humor, now seemed almost a flat gray. He looked at the broken-down mining machinery that still needed repair. He had hoped to have the repairs completed before dark.

No matter. The safety of his men was more important than any machine.

"How many?"

"Only a few, but the ringleader is one of the new hands that Jordan brought in. The one that wears the fancy holster tied low."

Hart mentally reviewed the new faces in the area. There were many who could be considered hired guns, brought in by Nelson Jordan. His enemy's move had left Hart no choice but to bring in some guns of his own. Hart had strength and courage. He had years of working in and around mines that had sharpened his mind and forged his muscles into bands of iron. He could also shoot as well as most Western men, but against a professional gunfighter he wouldn't stand a chance, just as his men wouldn't stand a chance. This particular gunfighter would be the one they called Parrish. He wasn't one of the best guns in the West, but he was still dangerous. And unfortunately, Hart did not have the kind of money it took to hire guns that were as fast and dangerous as the ones that Jordan had hired. At this point, it was still Hart and his men against Jordan and his hired guns.

The young messenger, Tom Tyler, was barely more than a kid. He was an honest, hard worker. Shannahan, an Irishman just a few years older than Tom, was a former boxer from the old country who had come to the New World to seek his fortune. Hart's other men were of the same type. In a fair fight, they could hold their own. But would they stand a chance against the men that Jordan was bringing in?

Hart continued to clench and unclench his massive fists as Tom watched anxiously. Hart knew that every second he hesitated could bring Shannahan that much closer to death. Jordan had done everything he could that was even close to legal to take over Hart's claims and meager mining operations. Now Jordan was raising the stakes with the gunfighters. It wouldn't be beyond him to kill Hart's men in cold blood, if that was what it would take to make Hart sign over his deeds.

Hart also knew that if he stood up to Parrish he might also be a dead man.

No matter. He hadn't mined and prospected for most of his life, finally finding the best vein he had ever seen, only to lose it to the likes of Nelson Jordan! Hart would die before letting that happen.

The older miner stood, reached for a well-used Winchester.

"Are you with me, Tom?"

"I'll follow you into the pits of hell itself," the younger man answered. "We all would. You know that."

"That just may be where we're headed," Hart answered grimly. "But if so, we'll go down fighting like hell!"

The sun setting beyond the dark hills cast coppery shadows on the two men riding leisurely down the well-rutted trail. In the distance, sounds of mining machinery could be heard and the burning odors from the smelter crowded out the natural smells of pine and night air.

"I'm not sure I like the smell of this town," Sam August Webster Two-Wolves said, laughing slightly. "I've smelled trouble before, but never an aroma quite like this!"

"I've seen some privies that smelled sweeter," Matt Bodine agreed, holding his nose with an exaggerated motion.

"Still, where there's mining, there's sure to be someplace for a beer. We've been riding long enough, I could handle the stink for a cool beer and a good card game."

"Ever the philosopher, Sam?" Matt said.

"I didn't spend those years in college for nothing!" Sam answered.

Both men laughed and continued their good-natured kidding. Though they rode leisurely, as if they hadn't a care in the world, each man kept his gun hand free. And their eyes constantly scanned the areas on each side of the trail, their ears listening for any sound that might hint of danger. They had been through many adventures and survived countless fights because of the caution that had become second nature to them and the easy way they worked together. They had learned from experience to always be prepared for any kind of trouble that might jump out at them from the next bend in the road.

The closeness of the two men came as natural as breathing for in truth they were blood brothers.

In the reddish shadows, the two men looked quite similar, as might be expected from brothers. Each was young, handsome, and muscular, over six feet tall and weighing over two hundred pounds. They were dressed simply, in comfortable clothes covered with trail dust. Around their necks each man wore identical multicolored stones pierced by rawhide in the Indian style. On a first, casual glance, they could pass for full brothers, and had many times.

A closer inspection, however, revealed a number of differences. Though both had a wild and reckless glint in their eyes, Matt had blue eyes and brown hair and Sam had black eyes and black hair. Sam's other features, however, had been inherited from his white mother. Only his cold obsidian eyes, which were occasionally softened with high humor, gave away his Indian heritage.

In spite of the different cultures they represented, the two young men were as much blood brothers as if they had the same mother and father. They were joined by knife and fire, and the Cheyenne blood-bond ritual brought them closer together than most white men could ever conceive or know.

Sam's father had been a great and highly respected chief of the Cheyenne, his mother a beautiful and highly educated white woman from the East who had fallen in love with the handsome Cheyenne chief and married him in Christian and Indian ceremonies. As boys, Matt had saved Sam's life. Though his home was on a nearby ranch, Matt had spent as much time in the Cheyenne camp when he was growing up as at his home on the ranch. He was finally adopted into the Cheyenne tribe, thus becoming a Human Being according to Cheyenne beliefs.

Sam's father, Medicine Horse, had been killed during the Battle of the Little Big Horn after he charged Custer, alone, unarmed except for a coup stick. When Sam's father realized that war was coming and that he must fight, he ordered Sam from the Indian encampment and to adopt the white man's ways and to forever forget his Cheyenne blood.

Matt and Sam had witnessed the subsequent slaughter at the Little Big Horn, though that was a secret only they shared. In the sad time that followed the battle, they decided to drift for a time across the rugged West to try and erase the terrible memory of the battle.

Though they looked like drifters, in truth they were well educated and wealthy. Sam Two-Wolves was college-educated, while Matt had been educated at home by his mother, a trained schoolteacher. Sam's mother had come from a rich Eastern family and left him with many resources, which Sam had used to his advantage. Matt had earned his fortune through hard work and smart business moves. He had worked riding shotgun for gold shipments and as an Army scout, saved his money, and bought land. Both Matt and Sam now owned profitable cattle and horse ranches along the Wyoming-Montana border.

The two men never looked for trouble, but neither did they ever back away from a fight, which caused them to be involved in many adventures.

And through their exploits, the two blood brothers were developing an unsought but well-deserved reputation as gunfighters.

As Matt and Sam continued to ride, they came upon the outskirts of the community itself. Dozens of tents had been erected, with a few ramshackle wooden buildings thrown in to break the monotony. At one point in the rutted road, a rough wooden sign had been nailed to a post. Toward the bottom of the sign was the name "Silver Creek." It had been crossed out, and a new name painted in: "Jordanville."

Sam pointed to the sign and suggested, "Seems the people of this town can't make up their mind about what to call themselves."

"It's not much of a town now," Matt answered. "Probably isn't even organized yet. You know how these new mining towns are. They pop up one day, and gone the next. I saw lots of these towns when I was riding shotgun."

Now Sam's keen senses picked up the smell of the river among the unpleasant odors of too many humans in too small of a space and the fumes from the mining operations.

The sound of the bullwhip was less subtle.

It cracked, and cracked again, piercing through the night.

The two brothers looked at each other.

"What do you think?" Matt asked. "Should we keep riding? It's not our problem."

"You know how I feel about whips," Sam said.

"Probably the only law here is by the gun. If we ride on in and take a look, we'll probably get ourselves involved in another fight."

Sam continued as if he hadn't heard his brother. His eyes had grown hard as he thought about injustices he had seen in his life. He said, "No beast or man should ever be subjected to that kind of shame . . . or pain."

"Oh, hell," Matt answered.

"You know how I feel," Sam said. "I just can't ride by and let any man or beast be bullwhipped."

"Yeah, I knew you were going to say that. There goes any chance for a quiet beer."

Even so, Matt smiled slightly to himself, for he felt the same way that Sam did.

Without another word, both men spurred their horses to greater speed toward the river, where the nasty sound of the bullwhip had come from.

CHAPTER 2

As Matt and Sam rounded the corner, there was still plenty of light to judge the situation. On the bank was a tall man dressed in a broad black hat. He wore two heavy revolvers in tied-down holsters and was holding a large bullwhip made of shiny black leather. The end was tinged in red from where it had torn flesh.

Just a few feet into the river, next to a long sluice used to separate gold from worthless rock, stood another man. He was tall and slim. He held no weapon except a shovel. He had been working without a shirt. Several small red welts oozed blood where the tip of the bull-whip had hit.

The man with the whip laughed. "Well, Shannahan, have you had enough yet to make you return to the old country? We don't need the likes of you or your boss here. If you take off now, I might let you live."

The man in the water said nothing.

The man in black waved his whip and laughed.

"On the other hand, there's too many damned Irish-men in Ireland as well. Might as well kill you now and be done with it."

On the riverbank stood many other men. Some of them wore guns and, like Parrish, had the appearance of hired guns. They laughed along with Parrish. Others wore plain clothes and had the look of simpler workers. Some of these moved restlessly from one foot to another, as if they wanted to help but could not. The majority seemed indifferent.

Shannahan finally crossed his arms against his chest, one hand still holding his shovel, and said plainly, "Parrish, you're a damnable coward."

Faster than the strike of a rattlesnake, Parrish flicked his wrist and the bullwhip cracked again. The Irishman tried to use his shovel as a shield, without success. Another red welt appeared, this one on his cheek. The man didn't flinch, however, even as the drop of red started to run down his cheek.

"I'd think twice about calling me names, son," Parrish replied, grinning broadly. "If I were you, I'd consider myself lucky that I'm just using the whip on you. If I really didn't like you, I would've already had a bullet through you. Probably several bullets."

The two blood brothers were still several hundred feet from the scene, but could clearly see and hear the exchange as they rode.

Matt sighed and said, "It's none of our business, you know. For all we know, that man in the river could have stolen the other man's wife. Or worse, he could have stolen a horse."

"You know better than that, brother," Sam said through clenched teeth. "We've both seen this scene too many times. You know what's going on as well as I do. And even if he did steal a woman, not even that crime is bad enough to be bullwhipped. Too many of my people have suffered that kind of fate. I don't plan to let anybody be bullwhipped if I can help it."

"Then I'm with you."

The two men had worked together long enough that only a few words were needed to develop a plan and put it into action.

"I'm going after Parrish," Sam said "You just make sure the others stay clear."

Shannahan briefly touched the blood trickling down his cheek, glanced at it, then turned his attention back to his tormentor.

"I speak only the truth," Shannahan said. "You're a damnable coward. Come out here and face me like a real man, and I'd prove to everybody here that you're not a man. Truth is, you know you'd stand no chance against me. You act brave, up there when you have the gun and whip and I have only a shovel. I'm calling you like I see it. You're nothing but a low-down, razor-backed cur of a mongrel bitch. I suspect that your owner, Jordan, is probably your bastard father. . . ."

Matt had to admire the way Shannahan was conducting himself. Though he knew he could be shot or crippled at any moment, he still stood his ground and tried to anger Parrish enough to make a mistake. It was a desperate gamble, one that Shannahan looked like he would lose.

Blood had flushed the face of the gunfighter. Parrish had angrily raised his hand to crack the whip with full force across the other man when unexpectedly he heard a horse racing toward him through the crowd. The spectators ran and jumped out of the way. Parrish looked up in time to see a grim face with dark eyes that were as cold as obsidian bearing down on him. Before Parrish could react, the other man reached out and plucked the bullwhip from his hand. In one fluid motion he threw the whip into the river and dismounted from his horse.

"Stranger, I don't know who you are, but you're a dead man," Parrish said.

"My name's Sam Two-Wolves, and I think I disagree with your assessment of the situation."

Sam's cool words, more appropriate to a drawing room discussion than to a potential shoot-out, made Parrish pause for another half second. It was enough time for Sam to cross the remaining several feet and connect with a solid right to the jaw. Parrish landed on his rear on the edge of the river. He was not hurt, except in his pride. He angrily jumped up to face the stranger.

Parrish waited for several seconds, confident that one of his men would help him out.

And then he waited for several more seconds. Still nothing, except for some low grumbles.

The seconds seemed like hours before Parrish took a quick glance to his left.

Another man that looked as if he could be a brother to Sam Two-Wolves was nonchalantly leaning against a tree, his revolver held lazily in his hand, while the other men were carefully placing their weapons in a pile in front of them. A few of them looked to Parrish and shrugged. Others in the crowd were smiling.

"You're on your own now, Parrish," Matt said.

"Let's see what kind of stuff you're really made of," Sam said. "Prove you're not a coward who needs a bull-whip to try to pretend he's a man."

Parrish turned back to face Sam. The gunfighter and Sam were about evenly matched in height and weight, but Parrish had his back to the wall. All eyes were watching him. He was the one challenged, and could not easily slip out of this fight.

"Well?" Sam continued. "What kind of man are you?"

Parrish suddenly took three steps and dove at Sam, driving his shoulder into the other man's belly. The gunfighter had telegraphed his move, however, and Sam had prepared himself by bracing his feet on the ground and tensing his muscles. To Parrish it felt like he was hitting a brick wall. Sam brought down a clenched fist on the back of the other man's neck.

The man in black staggered and dropped to his knees. As he fell, he reached out and grabbed Sam's legs and pulled. Sam was caught off balance, but managed to fall backward, away from the river. As he hit the ground, he kicked upward. The toe of his well-worn but polished boot caught Parrish in the chin, snapping his head backward.

The gunfighter, though dazed, caught himself and jumped back to his feet. He tried to stomp at Sam's groin. Sam moved, caught most of the force in his side, forcing him to gasp slightly. Parrish dove and tried to pin Sam. They rolled on the riverbank and both came up swinging. Parrish's fist moved rapidly, but each blow was blocked by Sam, who responded with a similar attack.

Though the two men seemed to be fairly evenly matched, Sam was in better shape. Parrish tired first. He let his guard down slightly and it was the only opening Sam needed. He took a quick step inside Parrish's swings and with a quick uppercut slammed his rock-hard fist into the gunfighter's chin. The crack of bone sounded loudly across the crowd and Parrish's eyes grew glassy.

Still, Parrish tried to come after him one more time. He was now quite slow and could not dodge Sam's final blow to the face.

The gunfighter started to slump to the ground. Sam caught him by his shirt collar, lifted him, and walked into the river toward Shannahan, who was watching the spectacle in wide-eyed amazement. Sam picked up the whip, now floating lazily on the surface of the river.

"My brother and I apologize for interfering in your business, but I have this thing about whips," Sam said in an apologetic tone. "Hope you took no offense."

"None taken," Shannahan said.

"Then that's settled," Matt said from the riverbank. "Let's go get a beer!"

"Good idea!" Sam agreed, dropping the gunfighter with a splash into the river, throwing the whip in after him.

As Sam and his new Irish friend waded back onto the riverbank, a small crowd of newcomers came into sight over a hill. In the lead was a large man. He was wearing no shirt and had specks of gray in his hair. Even in the fading light, his eyes shone with a fierce determination. Following him were several other men with similar expressions on their faces. A few carried guns. They all marched steadily toward the river.

"Have we got another fight?" Matt asked quietly. "We're outnumbered but could still take them on—"

"Oh, no," Shannahan said cheerfully. "It's just my boss, Clarence Hart, come to help me! Except you've already saved him the trouble!"

Sam and Matt stood side by side, where they could greet the newcomers and also keep an eye on Parrish, who was dripping on the riverbank and then stomping away from the scene. Others in his group were quietly retrieving their guns and disappearing into the night. Matt figured that he and Sam hadn't seen the last of Parrish, but that he would probably lay low for a while, at least.

Hart stopped in front of the two brothers, looked them up and down, and then glanced at Shannahan.

"Well, William McFey Shannahan, I heard you were

in trouble," Hart said. His voice was as big as he was. "I gather it wasn't with these two?"

"No, Mr. Hart," Shannahan answered. "I was in the river, doing my usual evening work for myself, as you encourage. And suddenly on the riverbank was that new gunslick, Jack Parrish. He had me with my pants down, so to speak, when up came these two and evened up the odds somewhat I have to thank. . . ." He paused and looked to Sam. "I don't even know your names!"

"He's Smith," Matt said. "I'm Jones."

"No, I'm Smith, and he's Jones," Sam corrected.

Hart raised one eyebrow at both of the two brothers, which caused them both to break out laughing.

"Oh, all right, you've got us," Matt said, grinning. "It's an old joke, anyway. My name is Matt Bodine. That is Sam Two-Wolves."

"I've heard of you two," Hart said.

Sam rolled his eyes toward the sky. He said, "I think I preferred the days when nobody knew who we were!"

"Fame is the price we pay for being good!" Matt said.

Hart ignored the wisecracks and said, "I've heard you're good with guns. Are you looking for work?"

"No, we don't need the money," Matt said. "We're just drifting."

"Besides, if we were looking for work, we're more the ranching type, not the mining type," Sam said. "I have better things to do with my time than dig in wet gravel. And I have an aversion to being underground while I'm still breathing."

"Mining's not the work I had in mind." Hart motioned to his men. "I've got some good men, some honest, hardworking men. But that won't be enough. I need a couple of men who are good with a gun. Trouble's shaping up, and I'll need all the help I can get."

"And you think we could do the job?"

"I don't want anybody to get killed, on either side. I just want to protect my men, and let them do their jobs. You handled that situation a few minutes ago real nicely. And nobody got killed. I like your styles."

"Thanks for the compliment," Sam said. "But we don't hire out our guns. We may fight if we think the fight's worthwhile, but it's never for money."

"We would be willing to listen to your story over a few beers," Matt added. "I have a feeling we walked into a hornet's nest, and it might be a good idea to find out more about what all the buzzing's about."

"We'll listen to your story, then decide if we'll stay around for a while or ride on."

Hart's face finally broke into a smile.

"In that case," he said, "the first round is on me!"